SURETTE'S BOOKS

Death and the Vagaries of Life in the French Quarter, New Orleans

Thomas Henry Bennett

I.

Darius Trémé twisted and released the lock. The heavy oak door flew open and the impact threw Darius Trémé aside. A tall, coal black phantom entered the house and stood over the boy; still yet surveying the boy's meagre frame; still yet seizing the boy's fecund imagination.

A hand gloved in black grabbed Darius Trémé by the arm, pinching and bruising his skin; holding him on tip toes; a hand clamped over his mouth - all the time Darius staring into the sable void between a velvet hood, aware of a scent he had known; a scent he could remember.

Suddenly, Darius was flung at the innards of the door - the door clattering hinge and mortise, shuddering as it banged shut. A large black canvas bag was slung into the adjacent living room, Darius being dragged behind with large powerful hands pulling him to; violence confusing him; absorbing him.

A punch split the boy's lip. Blood oozed slowly into Darius Trémé's mouth; blood mixing with saliva, sweetening and awakening his taste buds; rapidly coagulant blood nestling in the recesses of his lips. Darius had to force his body not to let itself go, tears welling in the corners of his eyes, pleading, begging - tears the precursor of harm - harm the obvious conclusion.

Duct tape was wrapped around the boy's head, sealing his lips; suffocating; stifling; silencing. Urine began filling his shorts and trickling down Darius Trémé's hairless legs, staining ochre the blood red carpet beneath, seeping without uniformity toward the recesses of the room. A second fist knocked him unconscious. Darius Trémé was now a malleable rump of whitened flesh; a compound of bone and sinew; expressionless; devoid of humanity; free of form; of meaning. His little body dropped to the floor, seduced by violence - limp - limp and spent.

Darius did not see a black canvas bag being unzipped. He did not see the rope, iron pulleys, chemicals, a large serrated knife and pincers - the latter two objects placed in the dancing flames of an open fire conveniently located at the centre of the room. Just a few thoughts flitted within as he fell back and forth, wrestling with consciousness, satiated by images of the beach, the playground, the park, his bike, the swimming pool, blowing out those seven candles on his birthday cake, kissing Mia Laval in the playground, being told off for being naughty, of being loved, of being Darius Trémé - an unremarkable seven-year-old boy.

Darius began coughing blood; congealed blood running down his nostrils, hardening on its release. As he coughed, he threw his rib cage forward. Something was holding him back; his freedom of movement restricted. He had to know how. He had to know why.

But Darius Trémé could not have known of a reef knot fastening a rope wrapped around his skull, restricting the movements of his head; of the purpose to the heat rising from the fire; of his nexus with each flame spitting violently below. Only when he saw the knife, did Darius Trémé try to understand. And only when he felt the heat of the knife, as its blood orange visage was waved a couple of inches from his eyes, did Darius lose all control, his bowels opening and watery excrement running unimpeded down the back of his legs, falling from his flailing limbs suspended six feet above the carpet. And only when Darius Trémé felt the passage of his innards run down his legs did he realise that he was naked; too petrified to understand; naked and too petrified to know that this was not a dream; naked and unknowing; oblivious; anomic; naked and discarded.

What did he know? What could he have known had he seen the architecture; the edifice constructed in honour of his demise? What could he have known of the architecture of a monster; the insidious design of the construct surrounding him; of the architecture of a mind? Darius Trémé was seven years old.

Traversing the entire length of the living room, dissecting it, was a horizontal wooden beam made of English Oak, twelve feet from the floor. At right angles were two smaller, horizontal trunks. To these were attached a number of ropes leading to the central trunk which looked down onto the fire and the hearth, then to another pulley and from the pulley to the floor. Darius Trémé was attached to the main beam, his legs bound at the ankles and his arms pulled to either side - cruciform; with a rope fixed firmly around his chest and a further rope tight around the boy's neck, suspending him by a complicated system of compensating pulleys, each dependant upon and controlled by the other.

Two clay pots sat above the fire. Mixtures were being stirred carefully, rhythmically and hypnotically. As they boiled each gave off a hideous vapour, filling the room with an acrid, bilious stench; a congregation of vapours brought to the boil returning Darius to full consciousness; sulphur and tar boiling upon the hearth, bubbling and smoking; intermingling; rising slowly and so infecting his nostrils; creeping into his lungs; a veil of nausea infecting and contracting the walls of his stomach. The putrescent odour was Darius Trémé's wake up call - his call to abide with the ritual about to unfold.

The knife was used first. A blade flashed before Darius Trémé's eyes before descending to cut Darius Trémé's right arm loose, leaving it to fall by his side. A deep, monotone voice told the boy to hold his arm out in front of him. Darius did so, lifting his arm, unable to stop his feeble, spindly arm from shaking.

Boiling sulphur was poured on to Darius Trémé's left hand. His skin began to blister, bubbling away and falling from his arm like liquid honey, unveiling the inners of his hand - tendon and bone; sinew and gristle; tissues burning for as long as there was oxygen to burn until all there was left was a stump at the boy's wrist.

Boiling black tar was poured over the stump, stopping the blood from pouring from Darius Trémé's veins. Red hot, black metallic pincers were used to pull skin from Darius Trémé's shoulders, exposing the bones of his shoulders and the ball joints at the top of his arm, to the air. Boiling tar was poured into the holes the pincers had left behind. The tar hardened quickly but not before metal clasps were inserted into the welts, attaching themselves to the inners of Darius Trémé's arms, with the viscose and sticky tar affording grip and mutating odour as it burnt Darius Trémé's skin.

The knife was brandished in front of Darius Trémé's eyes once more. His stomach was cut open, his large intestine removed, unravelled then left to hang, falling out of the boy's rib cage and all the way to the floor, until sulphur was poured upon the flesh - sulphurous burning flesh creeping slowly from the ground toward the boy's rib cage.

Finally, the knife dug into the boy's rib cage and the heart was removed, still beating. As the veins connecting Darius Trémé's heart were slit, the pulley holding the metal clasps which held up Darius Trémé by the neck and the arms, was disengaged and his body left to fall until the clasps and rope tightened, and his neck snapped, with Darius Trémé's limbs pulled from their sockets.

Blood now ran down the length of Darius Trémé's stiffening body, dripping from each limb and meandering toward what was left of his intestines as they hung from his sliced open stomach, falling half way between the boy's gut and the floor. Above, his shoulders were distended, horribly dislocated and contorted, seeking attention and failing to compete with the hideousness of his snapped neck. When Darius Trémé kicked in spasm, Darius Trémé's last act in life was the precursor of death. Now he held life no more.

One last act remained. A rag was dipped in the boy's blood and a rhyme was scrawled upon the pastel tones surrounding the hearth - the final statement of the assailant - black - black to the night, returning to the anonymity of the street and The French Quarter. All of the killer was all that was left behind. A message had been disseminated - the death of a minor and a message had been sent.

It was forty minutes before Darius Trémé was discovered, when his Mommy returned from work. It was a further forty minutes before Emma Trémé came to and realised that the flesh rotting above their living room floor was her sweet, lovely, innocent, seven-year-old boy, Darius - Darius Trémé.

Looking to the past was somehow for the future. Darius Trémé had been cut, hung, drawn and quartered and a sickness had extolled its vile nature in New Orleans. In the twilight of a life; a life lived in The French Quarter; an average life; a child who was neither a sage to be or discard, had been eviscerated.

As an English oak door slammed shut and the killer left in flight, with Darius Trémé dead and disregarded, Darius Trémé mutated into something other than a child. Over the following days few in New Orleans, Louisiana, a few were able to establish what he had become. Most would grieve simply for what he once was.

II.

Through coffee coloured glass; through the tarnished burgundy threshold of Whites, Doctor Roux Surette made a snap decision - White's fetid innards looked perfect - somewhere quiet; somewhere to reflect; somewhere, to think.

The most intimate table; Roux Surette chose the most intimate table. Needing a corner and a sense of protection, Roux Surette gravitated toward the darkest corner and the most intimate table - a sense of protection, without question.

Candlelight was a must. Unnatural light threatened and countered the ambient intimacy that made Whites unique amongst the jazz environs of The French Quarter, in the heart of New Orleans.

As Roux Surette sat down, falling clumsily into his seat, nausea began toying with his gut. A debilitating nausea was infecting both his body and his mind - what one human being could do to another; what one adult had done to a child.

Hunger? The surly waiter who passed him the menu had no idea how superfluous the menu was. Roux Surette acknowledged him and looked away. He needed a strong drink instead; a much justified moment of weakness.

A drink was placed upon his table - the passing value of Scotch its destructive glide through the soft flesh of the palette, sliding like molten lava through carbonised tissue to his innards. How Roux Surette needed pain when that Scotch caused his innards to fry. How he wanted to reject the contents of his stomach; how he hoped rejection would avail him of the contents of his mind.

Stretching down to his left he picked up his satchel, placed it on his table and began picking the lock. With its simple mechanism released, escape from consequence would be forbidden. A clasp flicked open; Surette looked inside, caressing the lip of a brown folder, noting the irony of the blood red ink titling the front cover.

'Darius Trémé: deceased. Preliminary Report.'

Very gently, Roux Surette started leafing the sharp edges of the report's slender pages. Touching those pages unveiled the remains of a child Surette's imagination had just escaped from. He knew what he would find in there. As with all such reports, the observer had to be objective, retaining a dry eye and attempted dis-association from the fragments of existence left by Darius Trémé.

Who could have attempted disassociation from the fragments of an innocent boy who was only seven years old? Who could have failed to be affected by the barbarity of the killer?

Touching those pages reflected every detail of the twisted and dismembered remains of a child, and every moment of pain that child had suffered - page upon page devoted to unveiled fact and sentence upon sentence conveying detail and detail conveying the last moments of a seven-year-old boy.

The tears of the author should have been spoiling the ink. As the ink ran into detail and Roux Surette started to read, his memory returned to the house where the body had been found and that desecration of innocence had began.

He remembered the tears of the uniformed officer outside. Those inside were trying not to look. Surette was told that the extent of the killer's insanity was hard to imagine, and, on seeing the body, imagination was ill suited to what Roux Surette too, had seen; to what Darius Trémé had suffered; to what Darius Trémé had been.

Returning to the present, Surette cast his eye around Whites. The stage looked barely lit and solemn; the floor was a match of dark, wooden chairs and tables singularly covered with candlelight - candlelight unveiling the profiled edges of peoples passing banality and waiting for the band.

Distraction and a crawling; a selfish, stealthy fear called him to take in and watch. What better than to avoid responsibility and follow the easy way out? What was easier than to forsake Darius Trémé and take the easy pickings from those all around?

They were tourists mostly. Each was at Whites to listen; to eat; to drink. Later they'd be investigating the sexual imperative, chasing their midriffs outside. This was New Orleans. New Orleans is about release and excess, thrill and deliverance. Tourists called New Orleans the locus of humanity. Surette called tourists, tourons.

Most of the diners were wasps smoking Cuban cigars, drinking cocktails and enjoying the Cajun menu. Randomly situated there were a few Afro-Americans smoking cigarettes, chewing cold fries and drinking bottled beer. They all seemed content and satiated, obliviousness being the bedfellow of success. The food looked good and the alcohol was plentiful - a cocktail suited to Surette's purposes of remaining in solemn isolation and a subliminal need to keep Darius Trémé away.

What better place than Whites? What better place than a tedious jazz club on turgid Bourbon Street, with its black and white stills of the greater jazz fraternity hanging off the walls; indiscriminately spaced photographs of jazz greats looking smugly down upon him - Armstrong; Basie; Gillespie; Davis; Ellington; Holiday; Brubeck; Coltrane. What was so attractive about music? What was so attractive about jazz?

The moment was fleeting. Surette had no relationship with music. If jazz was the norm, Surette was beyond the norm as a doctorate in psychiatry and several years at Harvard and a year at Oxford told him he was beyond the norm. Jazz was for the inarticulate; the intellect was the arena of the sane. Jazz was irrelevant and part of the fecund enigma of sound - the fecund enigma, of New Orleans.

Page one was a brief and disjointed synopsis of Darius Trémé's background and his last moments. Darius Trémé was of well-to-do French Quarter stock, his father a prominent businessman, his mother a Doctor. They lived on Governor Nicholls Street. School was local - the local French Quarter school for well-to-do French Quarter stock. Darius Trémé had left school at three thirty. It was a short walk home - just two blocks. Darius had walked two blocks and was seen letting himself in by a neighbour who saw nothing wrong. His mother found his remains just over two hours later.

Surette had received a call from the Chief of Police an hour and a half after that, and was asked to attend Darius Trémé's home to see what was left of the boy for himself. Surette's reputation had preceded him. As New Orleans most eminent psychiatrist and seemingly the only man in New Orleans qualified to engage and unveil the proclivities of the killer, he was asked to develop a profile of the mind capable of the annihilation of a child.

It was to do with a message, of sorts, scrawled in blood upon the hearth above which Darius Trémé had been eviscerated. It wasn't so much a note as a short rhyme - a cryptic justification and explanation for the evisceration of the body - what purpose the evisceration served and how it served the purpose of the killer. Initial police conjecture was that the killer was probably a local man; a specific type; a Caucasian; a psychopath; white and dysfunctional; probably a loner; probably insane.

But who didn't like to be alone now and again? What did dysfunctional mean? Darius Trémé was killed by a sick, white, male because Darius Trémé was an affluent, white, boy? Killers were predictable? Psychopathic killers were more predictable?

Surette considered how the New Orleans police force was so predictable. He remembered how inexact predictability was; how stupid inexact predictability was. And Surette considered himself.

His children attended Darius Trémé's school. His wife, Emily, was Darius Trémé's teacher. Darius Trémé was friendly with Alex, Surette's eldest boy. The Surette family lived in The French Quarter. Surette had always lived in The French Quarter. The Trémé family lived just one block away. Roux Surette was highly educated, respected, well known and affluent. So was Darius Trémé's father. Darius Trémé's father was a figure in New Orleans. So was Roux Surette. Roux Surette was a black figure in New Orleans - a black male in New Orleans. A black, male.

Sitting in Whites, Roux Surette pondered the significance of his skin, looking at his hands, rhythmically turning them over from white palm to black knuckle. Back and forth. Black, and white.

Race? Was this to do with race? Darius Trémé was a white boy. Was Darius Trémé tortured, eviscerated, ritualistically mutilated and murdered for being a white, boy? Was Darius Trémé forced to beg and plead for his life for being a seven-year-old, white boy?

Surette wanted to speak to Emily, his wife; he wanted to speak to his children. His mind was enveloped with questions and his body was enveloped with sickness. How did a child mutate into a man capable of killing a child? Why mutilate a child? What, as a parent, must one do right? What, as a parent, must one not do wrong?

From his inside pocket, Surette retrieved then extended his cellphone. The phone began to ring. A drummer brushed a snare. A saxophonist changed his reed. A double bass was plucked and strings of viscous spittle were ejected from a trumpet. Stage lights brought Whites to life and Roux Surette stepped outside.

Surette was seen by a television news team scouring The French Quarter and the New Orleans goldfish bowl had given up the man responsible for identifying Darius Trémé's killer. With no means of escape, Surette was standing in the doorway of Whites with a camera penetrating his eye line and a microphone penetrating his nostrils.

'Dr Surette; can you confirm that the nature of Darius Trémé's death was the most gruesome you have ever seen?'

'Can you confirm that Darius Trémé was not murdered sir, but executed?'

'Can you tell us sir, if rumours of a note detailing the killer's intention to kill others are correct?'

Surette obfuscated. Obfuscation annoyed him. Eventually he backed into Whites, noticing how quickly the manager shut the door behind him; how disingenuous the man became; how little he wanted him there. Surette's face would now be headlining the breaking news and Whites' tarnished burgundy doors would be providing the backdrop.

The New Orleans goldfish bowl he thought - a black may kill a black and little was ever heard. Darius Trémé was a dead white boy and a newsflash. An affluent white boy had been murdered and New Orleans was awake.

Surette apologised to Whites' manager when he realised that the Police Report was still open, still on his table and available to read. It could have been read. He thought he saw a figure move away from his table. Surette looked at the manager.

Had anybody read that document?

The manager shrugged his shoulders.

"Ladies and Gentlemen; welcome to Whites. We hope you have had a fine evening. If perhaps we could add to your evening, well we would be delighted to be of assistance."

Surette looked up and saw an over-gracious, semi-apologetic black musician.

"Ladies and Gentlemen; we have a fine act for you this evening; a fine act. You know this jazz - this art form of ours - jazz is not just American; jazz travels, ladies and gentlemen; jazz, travels. And tonight we will prove it. Back, by popular demand...."

A snatch at the cymbals; a beat on the drummer's bass drum. Trying to shuffle his papers away, Roux Surette tried not to listen. No big deal he thought - it was a band; another New Orleans band.

"Tonight, once more, from Oxford, England, we have the undoubted privilege to hear the silken vibe and cut-above sound of one unique horn. I want you to put your hands together for Will Chaucer. Put your hands together Ladies and Gentlemen. Put your hands together for Will Chaucer, ladies and gentlemen - Mr William, Xavier, Chaucer."

As Surette looked up, a white man appeared from behind the stage holding a battered brass trumpet; a thin, vaguely angular white man wearing a Stetson Hat which threw shadow over his senses and exposed only the corners of his jaw to the light.

The man smiled as the audience tittered, his perfect white teeth discernable through the smoke. Will Chaucer put the trumpet to his face; and the band looked at each other and smiled. Surette presumed Chaucer was about to blow his first note. He was. He did. Surette saw the windows vibrating. Intensity of tone and pitch pummelled his ears. All around the musical rejoiced at the purity of his sound; others rejoiced at the volume. Chaucer faded into darkness at the back of the stage.

Searching for distraction, Surette was a little intrigued. Five minutes passed and the Englishman remained in darkness. Surette grew impatient. Chaucer was making him wait. This apparent paragon of English eccentricity was making him suffer the indignity of a tease. But Roux

Surette had plenty of time; plenty to drink; plenty to occupy his mind. In any event, safety from the press outside was outlasting them within. The price was an evening with jazz.

With three minutes on the clock, Chaucer re-appeared, stood in the light, screwed up his face, smiled once more and began to blow a set which was such a working synthesis of Gillespie, Hubbard, Armstrong, Davis and Marsalis that Roux Surette had to listen; as all had to listen - just had to listen.

For sheer technical mastery alone, Roux Surette's ear was impressed, for all technical mastery was to be admired. Yet watching the glazed eyes of Whites' audience, Surette saw how far this man's music had made them travel - to the past; to the future? Why?

It was just music. To Roux Surette, music didn't matter. Only language mattered. Only language could articulate the pathological bent that had prefaced the hideous end of Darius Trémé; so only language mattered.

III.

Olivier Godin was thirty-four, an unmarried loner and an introvert; to some, a sodomite; to others, a leper, a discard, a disease; dismissed as a result, a result self-inflicted. Olivier Godin's life was innuendo; it was rumours - rumours of proclivity; how he ran toward the unnatural; rumours that he wasn't one to be mixing with women and that men were his thing; rumours that men were Olivier Godin's thing.

Hounded by the mongers of his sexuality, Detective Olivier Godin was an outsider, and Olivier Godin was nobody's fool. Random poison finds easy prey and the singular document placed upon his chair told him that he had been chosen, and he had been chosen to fail. Time had caught up with him, cornered him, claimed him for castigation then censure, and all of the snakes seeking the consumption of a runt now had their chance. They knew what had happened to Darius Trémé. They knew that no detective could possibly solve the case. The Darius Trémé case was one to miss, like bubonic plague, like cancer; for this was madness, not reason; for this was an undetectable, not a solvable crime. Their succour would be his departure, a broken man; a strange, unsolvable man; an unpleasant disengaged man about to be eclipsed by a riddle scribed in the blood of a seven-year-old boy.

Godin checked his emails. Only one message seemed relevant. At 7.15 a.m., Eveny Brien, the New Orleans Chief of Police, had left a message and he was duly summoned. Oxygen is sparse for lowly detectives in such rarefied air and when Godin took the lift to the top floor, knocking on her door then stepping inside, it had been a long day. And now, somehow, the ensuing attention could only preface the oncoming, unwanted ordeal.

Brien was a striking woman, certainly - with a bobbed crown of sable hair, a long and pitted nose and a thickening body. The size of her nose, the proportions of her head, the charcoal crest and the conclaves of flesh below were acutely exacerbated by a flawed chin-tuck coupling with eyelids desperate to crawl toward the upper curvatures of her ears - skin pinched and squeezed; pulled and punctured; gripped and tightened; stretched and cured. Her demeanour suggested cruelty; her physicality suggested misplaced vanity.

Godin wondered what more to expect as she carefully watered the cacti, azalea, rosemary, coriander and basil, placed upon her sill. Maybe silence was a ploy to test his security, or lack of it. Godin saw through it, and silence would not predicate his response and his brief and cruel examination of her outstanding physicality would not predicate his opinion. Brien sat down and raised her eye line until their eyes met.

"Rumour has it you are the best homicide detective we have."

Godin was silent; still.

"Rumour has it you are a homosexual."

If she was expecting a response, she didn't get one. Brien had either chosen to empathise with what she thought she knew about Godin's sexuality, establishing a rapport with a non-threatening male, or she had joined the throng to denounce him based on an unsubstantiated rumour.

"The Bible tells us most clearly that homosexuality is wrong. Sodomy is a sin. I will not have a man on my force threatening the discipline of my men. They tell me that all you do is solve crimes and look after your father. They are afraid of you because you won't indulge them; that you are queer; that you work alone and you keep yourself to yourself. Why should I retain a man bad for morale in a profession where morale is all-important?

They say you are the best we have. The head of homicide says you are the finest mind we can offer the people, albeit that he says it through gritted teeth. He wants to get rid of you. I can see you have an unblemished record; I can sense there is a great deal to you."

Brien smiled. Her indiscriminately spaced teeth were bleached white and clung to her gums like stalactites and stalagmites.

"It is unsubstantiated. I have no evidence of what you are. I have no need to know what you feel and who you indulge. But I will not have homosexuality within my police force. So; I have a dilemma. Well the choice has been made for me - a child; an affluent child, was murdered in The French Quarter last night. The minutiae of the death is unlike any I have seen before and the press are baying like bloodhounds for the killer, and if not the killer, for me. And you have been given the case."

Brien shuffled in her chair, cupped her jaw with her hands and edged closer.

"I am giving you a chance; just one chance. Solve this crime using any means you can - any trouble with the bigots, you tell me; any trouble with the head of homicide, you are to tell me. You are to report to me at all times and no one else. I will fend off the press; and you will have a free hand to run this any way you like.

Talk to the psychiatrist involved - Roux Surette. He has been asked to create a profile of the killer. Godin; remember the difference between fact and opinion. And be discreet. Use Surette but use him well. You have one chance. Solve this crime and I will protect you. Fail and you will be damned. Am I understood?"

Godin nodded. As he did so sunlight charged from behind a cloud and into his eyes until Brien blocked its path - Brien now a silhouette, unseeable and unknown.

"Results Detective; results."

Godin backed out of the room and returned to his office. Four feet from his door his ear caught the back end of another misinformed jibe about who and what he was. All he had ever wanted to do was serve. What concern was it to others how he wished to conduct his life? Through these skewed social mists, he wished he could see the summit, but all he found was denuded visibility and the perils of human nature conspiring to deny him a chance. The gradient was steep enough for most already so why he had been chosen to face the odds with a greater pack to carry? How could he be bad for morale when conjecture and bigotry had brought them all together?

Let them say what they like; let them deride; let them laugh at his expense, for only he knew what was within. But what were Brien's motives? She had shown no signs of empathy with a man who had suffered to excess; there were no excessive signs of aggression either. Yes; she fell on the Bible, whatever mangled edition she had chosen to use, but she did not say that she believed it. And she had given him a chance. Was she trying to get rid of him knowing blame could be posted his way if he failed, or was she hoping that he would succeed? Godin sifted through her words; he sifted through her actions. Finding few clues he resigned himself to the added pressure. Why was his sexuality an issue? Why?

The answer was clear as Godin read the Darius Trémé file over and over again and each sentence exposed the ritualistic evisceration and murder of a seven year-old boy. Godin knew why he had been chosen. The hideous death of the son of a prominent citizen had put the Police department under enormous pressure - why not place all of that pressure upon one head when failure was more likely than success? Why not seek out the weak link in the chain and exploit it, allowing the finger to be pointed and blame to take its place? This was a matter crying for a patsy. And a patsy they had found.

Godin would be unable to choose his fate by the utilisation of his mind and all of the skill, patience and learning that had made him the outstanding detective in New Orleans - doubtless, he would fail; doubtless, he would be fired; doubtless, the sniggers had commenced the moment he had been earmarked. Few would fail to be amused by the denouement of a suspect male, and few would care at his demise.

His only course of action was to be beyond reproach. Only then, could the logic of rejection not proffer his descent and so reach its unwarranted destination. But the precipice was just a small step away, and the wrong or the right investigation was just enough to send him over the edge. The Trémé boy was just a matter of time - a poisoned chalice; the gift of a biblical homophobe punishing him for the crime of not being seen as a womaniser, the apposite man and a lodestar for the mindless epithets of manhood. The moment the Darius Trémé file had landed on his desk; the moment Godin saw that innocuous brown folder, he had guessed correctly that he had been put forward as a sacrificial lamb and offered to the populace.

Why had Roux Surette been chosen to accompany him? Why, in The French Quarter, where madness and eccentricity breed and mutations of norms engender perversity, did Roux Surette stand out as an enclave of reason? Surette's reputation, brainpower and insight seemed perfect, for whoever had killed that boy had left some sort of conundrum; a challenge no doubt, for the fraternity of the mind; a challenge for the educated; a challenge not meant for the likes of a lowly detective to solve. Why place this high achiever amongst a man with no future? Surette would have been protected; why not now?

He put a call into Surette's office. Surette was with a patient and he did not wish to be disturbed. Strange; Godin wondered what kind of patient stood in the way of the Trémé investigation. But to wonder at all was all too often to be imprecise. Godin put conjecture to one side and decided to traverse The French Quarter in the direction of Darius Trémé's house. He had plenty to do there in any event.

IV.

Roux Surette had slept badly. All night, mutations of recollections had mingled with fear, and the secret meanings of dreams had danced and flirted inside his head - recollections of the night before; mutated recollections of Darius Trémé; mutated recollections of the twisted mind, of a killer.

He decided to take a shower. If he looked down, his nakedness seemed apposite. If he looked up, scalding water pounded his face while furtive clouds of choking steam cloaked then softened his body. Whether he looked up or down, the heat brought pain and with that pain, the iniquity of the night before should have been evicted.

No matter how he tried to evict his feelings, physical pain proffered little escape from the suffering within, as he tried to piece, categorise and sift through structures of emotion the sight of Darius Trémé's body had erected. But difficult urges of solace mixed with the drive to have the killer trapped and exterminated, and the anger of retribution mixed with the lethargy of mourning. But Surette could ill-afford lethargy; and responsibility denied him mourning. All mourning would have to be deferred. And so, too, would this resurrection of a private despair.

For Roux Surette was always the object of other's despair. His latent choice was the eviction of feeling in search of understanding others; into unveiling personality, motive and trying to establish the connections and pathways to the mind, sifting through the sum totals of past peoples to establish a present pattern and getting a type, a manner, a social-proclivity-set possibly giving clues to the identity of the patient, or a killer.

His thoughts turned to his children. Alex and David would be coming to terms with loss for the first time. How would grief manifest within and manipulate a child - his child - immediacy; incredulity; the manifestation of disbelief - gravitation and changes; changes that needed to be watched. But Surette rarely saw his children, so rarely could he watch. He just wanted to be close to his kids; urges to touch and hug them; urges to hold, to touch and to hug his wife, his wonderful wife. He wondered whether Emily had heard the news. But the off-chance of Emily's knowing was small, for the previous evening Emily Surette would have put the children to bed and read a book, a novel, or a play. Again, Surette wondered about the kids, as stray thoughts tugged and pulled his abstemious bent - a concerned father and a continent mind; chalk and cheese; black and white; alive, and dead.

And now the day needed chasing - his daily lot a relationship with a veritable litany of well healed problem extollers looking for wisdom, clarity and answers upon the psychiatrist's couch – his daily lot directing the well-to-do New Orlean populace with their need to extol, define, decry, deliver, dismiss and denigrate everything from a husband's toupee to the criminal extremities of sexual degeneration; each and every day unveiling the most puerile neuroses to the most complicated constructions of self-justification and avoidance - each patient different; each patient having their own particular and unique needs, from the transparent to the grotesque to the mainliner with cash and curiosity. The question always the same - why? The answer usually the same - it depends. There were, no answers - just curiosity - curiosity and no answers.

Roux Surette was, at the very least, curious. There lay his secret as a good psychiatrist. Roux Surette searched for nothing in himself. His was an unencumbered search for the pathological wanderings of others - the nemeses in all of them; solutions for all of them; and never any answers for any of them.

Still he couldn't shake Darius Trémé from his mind, comparing the mechanic of the boy's death to the sights on the wards of the New Orleans University Hospital - the grotesque of the external - bullet, blade, bottle, glass; the grotesque of the internal - cancer, cirrhosis, stroke. Commonality; melanoma was more often than not self-inflicted, arterial thickening the same. Gunshot was often the result of a gunfight, probably over drugs - bullet, blade, bottle and glass - anything from an alcohol-led brawl in a French Quarter bar to a savage encounter with a jealous husband. And there were many jealous husbands in New Orleans.

"You have only one consultation this morning. Strange accent really. Didn't really sound messed up like they normally do; didn't seem nervous. He sounded rather normal."

Normal men sat on Surette's couch every day of the week, unaware of their status as normal; unaware of the meaning attached to dress, voice, manner - guilty lawyer, neurotic housewife, timid accountant, unfaithful banker, latent homosexual, diffident mother, errant father, abhorrent dad. Surette had listened to half of the high flyers and most of the low flyers in

New Orleans, sitting through garden variety dross of heightened self proclamation; of people who thought of themselves as different, weak, strong, hard, soft, stupid; all in some way losers in a non-zero sum game; all of them looking for answers. And Surette gave them answers. Surette got rich giving them answers, although money wasn't Roux Surette's thing. Neither were answers.

Surette wondered if he had a name. His p.a., Quinn, looked embarrassed.

"Refused to tell me. Said he would rather disclose his name to you. It didn't seem odd; it sounded appropriate. I'm sorry. But there really was very little opportunity to object."

Momentarily confused, Surette closed his study door behind him and placed his satchel on his desk, strumming its lock and clasp - Darius Trémé back on his mind; Darius Trémé mixed with reflections of Emily, the children, Darius Trémé's parents, his parents, his future and reactions within the close French Quarter community now riddled with the misery of incumbent fear. He had the responsibility to placate and assuage that fear. Surette knew that Darius Trémé would not be the only one. No man who had left such a convoluted testament to his insanity would be content to set an urge aside as if a switch had suddenly been flicked off.

"There is a gentleman in reception waiting to see you."

Surette moved his satchel to one side. Underneath was his daily copy of the Times Picayune. Its headline hit him like a bullet from a gun.

"Child Killer in the French Quarter. Darius Trémé, seven years old, executed yesterday...a cryptic note left behind...a warning...more are to follow...Doctor Roux Surette, the prominent New Orleans psychiatrist, called in to assist with enquiries...Doctor Surette 's analysis pivotal...."

V.

Treading carefully, Olivier Godin ducked under the plastic yellow incident tape crossing the doorway of Darius Trémé's home, walked toward the living room and the area where Darius Trémé was found. On his way, he looked at the furniture skirting the Trémé's hall and the Trémé's decor. He noted how wealthy the Trémés were and recalled that nothing had been stolen, moved or disturbed. Robbery certainly wasn't a motive - this, clearly, wasn't a crime of economics, class, poverty or jealousy.

Godin considered Darius Trémé's parents. His mother's movements were accounted for. Darius Trémé's father was out of town. Darius was their only son. By all accounts, they were honest and decent people. Godin ruled out their involvement. Who, after all, would kill their offspring? Who could, kill their offspring?

Godin entered the living room. The room was basic and square, panelled on all sides by heavily varnished oak. The focus of the room was a stone fireplace and at the centre of the room was a large, square, glass-topped coffee table with beech legs each carved with a representation of a lion's head with a wooden mane flowing to the floor.

The coffee table was covered with the boy's congealed blood. Below, the floor was matted and soaked with blood, which had wrestled with the air and gone ruddy brown. A stench of sulphur infused the air. Above, two-thirds up each wall and two-thirds between the blood soaked ochre carpet and the ornate covings and carvings counter pointing high ceilings, seven or eight wooden beams traversed the room, with one beam in particular, bisecting the square. It was from this beam that Darius Trémé's body had been hung.

Godin continued walking the room, looking, absorbing and trying to let the environment filter into his mind - an examination Godin considered important. Too often, he had attended a scene of crime decimated by numbers traipsing in and out attempting to establish their particular theory as to death - theories of the most backward kind - the kind of basic and wildly inaccurate theorising so beloved of the New Orleans homicide department.

Godin berated his colleagues for being there first. This scene of crime had been disturbed by uneducated amateurs he had to work with - stupid men charged with trying to deliver retribution and deterrence to the community; men who didn't know what retribution and deterrence meant; guys just doing a job; guys blasé about death; guys blasé about life.

Careful where he put his feet, Godin stood underneath the very beam from where Darius Trémé's body had dangled. For a few moments, he tried to imagine the boy in the last throws of life, urine trickling from his penis, running down the insides of his pre-pubescent legs and mixing with loose faeces and blood dripping onto the coffee table below.

He swallowed hard. Instinctively, he shuddered. Pain was difficult enough to establish within the psyche of an adult; it was impossible to imagine the gravity of suffering the boy had endured or the miniscunality of his understanding, as the killer stood in front of him and watched him die.

Godin stood back for a moment. White chalk circles marked the floor behind him, circling the area where the boy's intestines had been found, ripped from his stomach by a knife. An indiscriminate part of the boy's intestines had been burnt while the child was still alive - part of his intestines burnt; part of them left to hang from his stomach while the boy was forced to watch. Officially, the cause of death was asphyxiation. The actuality of dismemberment invoked differences.

Using red-hot pincers, left at the scene, flesh had been torn from Darius Trémé's arm and thighs. A hand had been burnt away to a stump. On those places were his flesh had been torn away, the killer had poured a mixture of boiling tar and sulphur. His tongue had been pulled out and each of his limbs had been yanked from their sockets by the use of a pulley rigged around the boy's body. Finally, Darius Trémé's heart had been removed. It was unclear whether the heart was taken out while the boy was still alive. Godin had read that in Africa one form of punishment is to cut out the victim's heart, show it to the victim, slit the connecting veins, then eat the victim's heart for the adrenalin it possesses. Darius Trémé's heart was not eaten - it was removed, the connecting veins slit, then, using a hammer and an iron nail, banged into the beam from which Darius Trémé was left hanging. Scrawled in blood above the hearth was a cryptic rhyme.

The Preliminary Report did not say was whether Darius Trémé had been forced to strip. There were no signs of sexual assault; no signs that the attack was sexually motivated; no signs that an earthly desire had been involved. No, the killer's lunacy lived in some degenerate flip side; in some degenerate ether.

Godin concluded that involving Roux Surette was the right thing to do. He also concluded that Darius Trémé was irrelevant. A child was killed because he was a boy of seven years. And that was that. The point to his death lay in the reasons that a child had to be killed - a child and not an adult.

Still feeling nauseous, Godin departed. Apart from his original intention to expand his knowledge of how and where the boy had died, he decided there was little to be established from the scene of the crime other than basic locality. Time had skipped away from Darius Trémé's house and the intentions of his killer. The question was whether the point would be made again and how quickly.

He wondered whether picking a child was an easy picking. Maybe an adult would follow. Most killings were opportunistic or related to the prevailing economics of despair - violent spouses; drug peddlers; cheap economic crime and a criminal unable to clarify his motives and firing anyway - murder conducted via basic emotion or through the failing of the human condition. Murder was not complex - money, rivalry, contempt, hatred, drugs, alcohol, recklessness, capitalism, nurture, nature; the act of murder was often a simple lineage from anger to fruition - a spouse would die; a dealer was shot; a baby was suffocated. The distance between thought and action was short, embedded in emotion and the inability to control. Godin had seen all variants on every homicide he had ever worked and elements of each in different proportions in every crime he had been asked to solve in the last ten years.

In a gun death within the Projects, at least he could see motivation, and in a sibling killing, he could see that years of systematic rape and abuse could twist a woman's head and the husband would die. In a sense, these were understandable - the same ingredients - rivalry, fear, contempt, abuse, hatred; all somehow confused; somehow aligned with helplessness; aligned with greed, longing, desire. Or were they? And was such understanding his job anyway?

That job belonged to Roux Surette. Godin doubted whether Surette's experience lent him toward knowing the kind of mind who had killed Darius Trémé. The issue lent itself to precisely how he was going to deal with Roux Surette. The man was rather elusive, or seemed to be. The only time Godin had ever seen him or hear him speak was the previous evening, when Surette was interviewed live, outside Whites. Surette gave no definitive impressions. And as Olivier Godin got home, he wondered whether any definitive conclusions would come from the man, either.

VI.

"Doctor Surette?"

Surette looked up.

"Doctor Roux Surette? You are Roux Surette?"

Surette recognized him immediately - the voice; a manner; an outfit; his face.

"Look; you are Roux Surette, are you not?"

Surette watched the man smirk - a look of knowing; superficial insight - probably more to do with simplistic intuition.

"Presumably my face, this face, my face was not the face you wanted to see this morning. I am here, to help."

Pride; arrogance tightened Surette's chest. He offered Will Chaucer a seat.

"The couch; pray the couch - here to rid me of all of those ills your mind is anticipating - bog standard neuroses perhaps - contrition, longing, curiosity, exposition? I assure you I am not here for my benefit Doctor; I've had enough psychiatrists to deal with; to sit and deliver my mind on a platter, to you?"

Was this a lecture of sorts or one man's self-righteous justification for the contents of his head? Proud people sat on the couch all of the time. Many declared their sanity at the beginning - how they didn't need help; how they didn't want help. Breaking that particular façade usually took about an hour.

Surette tried to size the Englishman up. Will Chaucer was young, about thirty but a young thirty, with black hair, blue-green eyes and pallid, unsullied skin - rather small features on a square jaw, he thought, and handsome - Irish features perhaps, with conclaves of freckles spotted chaotically across his cheeks and over the bridge of his nose; a surreptitious grin; wild eyes; intelligent eyes; a presence certainly.

The excitement in Quinn's voice now made sense - a handsome Englishman was in The French Quarter notwithstanding the mystery and the self-evident, if rather basic charisma. Surette decided to ask Chaucer about his Englishness. It was strange to find an English musician in The French Quarter, let alone such an odd one.

"Is this curiosity or clinical inclination? The newspapers are very generous about your reputation. For the United States of America, you are a highly educated man - all the more remarkable when I look at the colour of your skin. I even understand you spent some time at Oxford. I'm an Oxford University man myself - three years at Merton College; law, if you must know, which is the dullest subject in Christendom - three long years watching honest children turn into obtuse, emotionally retarded walking, living, breathing, cadavers.

Englishness; my Englishness; born English; English parents; English public school; infused with Englishness; carried in my chest next to my pulse; Englishness infects the very marrow of my bones, to coin a phrase."

The man was intelligent, though a difficult type of intelligence to pin down. There were at least two voices already - a practical recognition of the elemental and a cynical overview of the same.

"That boy, Darius Trémé, was the first. I wouldn't insult your intelligence and assume that the killer is finished."

For the first time, Will Chaucer took the smirk off his face.

"Take my word for it Doctor - Darius Trémé was simply a taste of things to come."

Attempting to un-nerve Chaucer, and somewhat touched by his arrogance, Surette turned and looked at the academic certificates covering the wall behind his head. Chaucer noticed.

"You sit there day after day and pontificate to the vulgar masses am I right? Go see Doctor Surette and extend to him the benefit of your stupidity. Let him grapple with a non-issue and sort you out - pills, prescription, prognosis; expensive for sure but see him and you will be healed - money an irrelevance; a sense of person; a sense of being all that matters to the various wage slaves, gutter dwellers and scabrous detritus who waddle through that door and park their burger butts upon this tarnished couch."

Surette suggested cynicism.

"Not cynicism Doctor, but honesty. Honesty is the biggest faux pas in the contemporary world and compromise is all, rather compromise is somewhere between all and nothing."

Another cheap prophet; and Surette grew bored. He suggested a compromise. While the incumbent seemed content to waste his time for an hour or so, Surette decided to try to find out a little bit more about him.

"I bore you? Why? Have you ever had to come to terms with tragedy, suffering and the kind of personality misuse you pretend to come across every day you sit in that chair? Why does a trip to Harvard and Oxford give you the right to guess? All you do is prostitute the books you have read, then play upon the weakness and stupidity of others. Take last night - most people who turn up when I play, leave with a little appreciation for the sounds they hear. You only saw; you never heard. I watched you from the stage looking sullen, lost, tired, drawn; I saw you mixing with the reporters outside and I saw your face on the cover of a newspaper this morning. One may have thought music appealed to you last night more than any other. One may have thought of jazz as the ideal preparation for the difficulties you are about to face."

Obtuse, sufferance, obscure, difficulty, sullen, lost, tired, drawn - Chaucer knew how to get under a man's skin. Surette drew breath at how this man had the potential to get under his skin. One question stuck in Surette's mind - why would Chaucer predict difficulties? He felt imperilled to ask.

"I was wondering when the penny would drop."

A smug self-congratulation covered every syllable emanating from Will Chaucer's mouth. Surette felt annoyed; and little was he ever annoyed.

"Cast your mind back to the moment when you returned to Whites and realised that details of the Trémé murder had been left on your table next to the heady and deserved Scotch you ordered for a semblance of comfort. Remember - a figure in the darkness; a figure recognising your return?"

Surette was none the wiser.

"Lucky for you Doctor; lucky for you that I had the fortune of reading the very report I imagine you wanted to keep to yourself. Lucky for you I read the New Orleans Police Report describing the manner of the boy's death."

The penny, dropped.

"Terrible. Taste shall we say. Whoever did that has a taste for it. It will not stop at one. This killer has a point to make. And I can tell you why."

Intrigued by the cheek of the man, Surette wanted to know why. Chaucer was magnanimous.

"Experience - a small word with a myriad of meanings; a way of looking at the world based on matters known personally and encountered within; not the surrogate world you live in but recognition of action, circumstance and meaning; a way of rationalising events and coming to terms with them; a way of establishing meaning that gets relayed through discourse with relevant others - one to listen and suggest and the other to deliver. What I want is to assist and help you create a pathological profile of the monster that killed Darius Trémé.

I read the note left by Darius Trémé's body. The note is a riddle, a challenge and a conundrum; and was put together to test and examine whoever is put in charge of the case. Then there is the body itself. There are reasons why it was mutilated and a purpose to the wounding; and not necessarily to inflict pain on Darius Trémé. The ritual nature of the boy's death was far removed from Darius Trémé. The nature of the killer lies in what was done to Darius Trémé - the boy remained utterly innocent until the moment he drew his last breath."

Surette remained impassive, his mind working in different ways. Listening to Chaucer had helped him establish one thing - the Englishman was interesting and perceptive, even if deluded and in some ways, rather trite.

Surette considered his interest in getting to know him - where Chaucer come from; how he thought; what he was referring to when he talked of the value of experience. Then there were the alternatives ways of looking at the man. Chaucer could indulge in blackmail any time he wanted to. It was just one anonymous call to the press, passing himself off as an insider on the Darius Trémé case and disseminating details of the message left at the scene. The possibilities were endless. Certainly, he had to assume Chaucer had worked out the possibilities for himself. Whether he liked it or not, Will Chaucer was already central to the Darius Trémé's case - as central, it seemed, as he was.

Surette wondered whether he could he extract something of Will Chaucer for himself. It was a reasonable suggestion, for Chaucer's protestations of experience were just so. Surette needed to establish the value of Chaucer's claims - after all, Chaucer was telling him that he knew how the mind of the boy's killer worked on the basis of his own background. Was Chaucer telling him that he had a kind of sibling empathy with the perpetrator of this hideous crime?

How was it going to be possible for Will Chaucer to back up his arguments unless he too, had some kind of relationship with a mind disposed toward killing a child? He needed an answer. Chaucer laughed out loud.

"Sitting here and trying to help you is hardly the actions of a killer; not that the killer is exactly rational in the terms you and I understand. Still, even I am not cruel enough to try to outwit you while you stand without the appropriate tools at the coalface of this investigation. The grounding for the idea is feasible, although the suggestion itself is ridiculous."

Surette tried another tactic.

"This is not about vanity. This is about retribution for the loss of one boy's life and the need to stop anyone else from getting hurt. It is also about good fortune. If I had not read your papers last night, I would not be here now. If I were not here you would still be here in a month's time with blood on your hands."

Surette wondered whether Will Chaucer knew that his own children attended Darius Trémé's school; that he knew the boy and his family; that his wife was Darius Trémé's teacher. It was as if Chaucer could read his thoughts.

"That your children attend the same school? That your wife teaches there? It is the sort of detail newspapers thrive on. Let me see - Doctor Roux Surette, native of New Orleans, father a decorated soldier, mother a nurse; married for eight years; first child born out of wedlock, second child legitimate - happily married; the quintessential American dream; the type of family unit preachers seem to want to establish at every turn of their bastardised interpretations of the good book; a political quest-point; a politician's lodestar. The newspapers have you down as some sort of answer to all evils. One can only assume you are the answer to all evils because the majority of The French Quarter's untermenschen have sat upon this couch."

Chaucer was right. In the years he had spent listening to the New Orleans community bare their collective weaknesses Surette had built up a stock of knowledge within a community that had built its own stock of reliance upon his advice. There was not an especial person in Louisiana who hadn't paid him a visit.

"In return for my assistance you want me to give you personal information upon which you will assess my credibility? What I tell about myself will allow you in your vast inexperience to make a judgement upon my reflections as to the nature of the sick individual that murdered Darius Trémé. You will therefore make a judgement on the veracity of my claims based on what - presumably the veracity of your knowledge? You do not have any sort of relevant knowledge therefore you cannot make a judgement on the veracity of my comments. I like the stupidity of your reasoning. In honour of your stupidity, I will comply with your request but on my terms. These terms are simple.

I will sit on this couch and offer myself to you each morning. In the afternoon we forget my personal monologue and set about trying to focus upon, identify and catch this killer before another child dies."

Surette didn't expect Chaucer to agree. Chaucer seemed only too happy to let his past speak for itself. Chaucer seemed to be a challenge. Roux Surette accepted the challenge notwithstanding Darius Trémé, or, in addition to Darius Trémé. And, without regard his claims of honesty, which Surette thought odd given that Will Chaucer could well be a litany of obfuscation and duplicity, any man comfortable with the idea of speaking of one's very personal secrets was going to be a challenge, because the mind learns of to segregate secrets and keep them to oneself.

"Let me assure you that there is simply no point being dishonest. You need to establish whether I have one ounce of credibility and I will cooperate and try to accommodate you in any way I can. This morning I will let you treat me as one of your patients and this afternoon we will concentrate on the rhyme left by Darius Trémé's side."

For a few moments, Surette relaxed and silence passed between them. Chaucer looked distracted. He walked toward a window and looked down upon Royal Street.

"You have company."

Surette followed Chaucer to the window. A number of journalists were milling on the pavement below.

"It seems as if answers are expected straight away. You haven't got to work yet and people want answers. People always want answers."

Looking down, Surette realised that until Darius Trémé's killer was found, he had become public property.

"You have little time to impress, Doctor. Would you like to leave instructions with your receptionist as to the appropriate way of dealing with these vultures?"

Surette called Quinn. He told her that no one was to disturb him. When he returned, Will Chaucer was back on his couch.

"Right Doctor; what do you want to know?"

VII.

As far back as he could remember, Olivier Godin had wanted to walk in the footsteps of his father. But now that Jack Godin was mute and incontinent, with his body imprisoned in a wheelchair, and his brain incarcerated within his body, the only interaction between Olivier and Jack Godin was Godin's daily summary of his life on the New Orleans force.

Jack Godin's deterioration had been rapid. Although Parkinson's disease had left no intellectual deficits, Parkinson's disease deceives the misinformed and makes the observer believe that the mind is as moribund as the body. Jack Godin last spoke some years ago, and for the love of his father and in some senses, to keep things the way they had always been, Godin continued their relationship as if conversation was two-sided and mutually beneficial. As to whether it was, the answer lay in questions of spirit beyond the simple mix of chemicals and water representing mere form. Olivier Godin could see, in his father's eyes, a life force as strong as it ever was; a life force beyond the simplistic biological. And as long as

Godin could see understanding, interest, appreciation and human spirit itself, he would continue their relationship as if nothing had happened to cut this man off from the agency his body provided for his mind. Jack Godin still represented an outlet for his son; Olivier Godin still represented an outlet for his father.

So, holding up the Preliminary Report in front of him, Olivier Godin started to read aloud, pausing now and again, stopping intermittently to emphasise facets of the document, making sure his father picked up every word. Afterward he remained silent, concerned that his father had absorbed the information while he stood and walked the room, his father's lifeless façade provided an obvious and disconcerting counterpoint to the energy his son exuded.

"I have been given this case. I, alone, have been given this crime to solve."

With every word Godin spoke, his demeanour changed. Gone was the stiff and controlled awkwardness of the morning; gone was the self-styled physical repression Godin had grown into as he comported himself at work. With his father he was free; with his father he could discuss and develop his ideas, embellish his feelings and manner away from the constricting subliminal overtures of the department - his arms fell loose by his side; he became animate; his voice modulated and ran up and down scales to a range many tones higher and many tones lower than the restrictive fifth he reluctantly demonstrated in the office.

"We have a new Chief of Police - a woman by the name of Eveny Brien. She gave me the case personally; the first time I have met her. She called me in to her room this morning and threatened me on suspicion that I was a homosexual; that I was bad for morale and a disruptive influence. I was given an ultimatum - solve this murder or the homophobes will be free to feed upon me.

I know what she is doing. The stakes in this inquiry are so high that they have decided to make an example should they fail. She said she would protect me if I solved this case. I keep thinking about the political machinations of the department and her relationship with the powers that be. What has she to gain from my success when I am a pariah? Does she really want to see a good Detective and a dedicated and loyal Detective, get on and achieve because that is best for the people we serve? Or is she just dangling a carrot in front of me knowing that my failure will give her the excuse she needs to see me run out of the job?"

Olivier Godin stopped talking and looked at his father, searching for recognition. His love for his father blinded him. The way he felt was sequestered by his mouth, fell into his father's ears and the answers filtered from his father's eyes back into Godin's mind. Save that they never. Jack Godin was impassive and inert. And Olivier Godin never saw the exercise for what it was - myopic love creating a one-sided sounding board. The process, to any other, would have seemed fruitless, save that it wasn't fruitless - not to Olivier Godin.

"So I have to find the animal that has killed this boy. But this is unlike anything you or I have witnessed before. I have just been to the little boy's house and seen for myself what was done to him and where it was done. I have never encountered such a calculated and carefully planned execution of a small child who was the enemy of no one. I mean this was an innocent little boy.

You always taught me the value of detail. There is nothing here that would give the slightest clue as to the identity of the killer. This is evil beyond the normal parameters of expectation. The autopsy report is unlikely to give anything away and my fear is that forensics will be a dead end. Past transgressors are likely to be of no use because they are all locked securely away and the type of mind capable of this crime would have been anomalous and exposed long before now. So I have nothing to go on which is anything other than intangible and I have very little idea were to start. I have been given this case because it isn't going to be solved. Eveny Brien knows it, the homophobes know it and the more I think about it, I know it too."

Godin took a Marlboro from his pack. As he struck a match, he pushed his father's wheelchair through the living room, through the French doors and into the adjoining courtyard.

"She wants me to liaise with this psychiatrist, Roux Surette. She says he is amply qualified to develop a composite psychological analysis of the killer. My feelings are ambiguous. I cannot see how this could do any harm; but I cannot see how one would make the jump from a tick list of behavioural traits with a killer of this type, and getting a conviction.

It is coming up to lunchtime and I haven't even spoken to the man yet. He seems to be with a patient and will not be available until that consultation is finished. What kind of a man puts pill poppers and bored females before the investigation of a crime as heinous as this? A killer with this kind of disease will not stop at one. There are going to be others. What kind of man is willing to jeopardise his career, listening to the mealy words of an inconsequential when other innocent children may die? What kind of man is that?"

Satisfied his father was as comfortable as he could be, Godin decided to leave and walk through The French Quarter, back to Police headquarters on Dauphine. It was another extremely humid day. How the humidity of the South asked questions of temperament. How easy it was for the heat and claustrophobia of The French Quarter to choke a man's mind. How quickly nerves frayed; and how quickly The Quarter's regularly irregular absurd plant-pot people lost control. The weather had been steadily getting hotter; and the humidity was rising. Could the weather be the catalyst that had caused Darius Trémé's killer to flip?

Godin smirked at the absurdity of the idea. The French Quarter was a magnet to absurdity - a tapestry of insanity yet the locus of life. How Godin enjoyed The Quarter; how he valued life - The French Quarter; a lodestar to all the maladjusted, oddballs in North America. Legend had a curse on the area, but the curse wasn't supposed to behave as an attractant to all manner of crazy peoples there to feed, gorge and gestate on the insanity of each other - contrast the creativity of man, the character of crime and the multifarious ensemble of peoples who descended upon The French Quarter and gave it life. How nature and the infinite varieties of humanity conspired to produce an infinite number of motives so producing an infinite number of outcomes in one place. As he looked at the passers-by on Dauphine - tourists and locals; locals distinguished by their eccentricity and more often than not, their earthy and relaxed sense of humour, he tried to understand how a party town such as this could erect such hedonistic moralities standing for the delightful and inspirational side of human nature.

Then he thought of the dark and sinister pathology of a man capable of killing a child - reasons to laugh and reasons to kill were everywhere, from the fresh faced enthusiasm of The Quarter's new arrivals soon to turn into old stock, riddled with alcohol, cigarettes, drugs and cul-de-sac expectations, to the die-hard many resigned to suffer the self destructive tendencies of an area where a weary lack of expectation fell hand in hand with the ability to obliterate oneself with moral impunity. Proof was all around. Was it any wonder that the gentle balances of constitution weighed on French Quarter scales attended the dull thud of outcome as the scales of fortune loaded the populace with perverted desire? How The French Quarter was ripe for the desecration of innocence. How the economics of despair and the apparent façade of inner wealth juxtaposed the meaningless lives of the majority. It wasn't hard to imagine where the killer came from. Potential killers were on every doorstep and in every bar.

VIII.

Surette decided to put matters into context. Psychiatry is often presented as an excursion into the past of the adult; and more often than not the rules look to deep-set trauma in the adult commencing in the adult as a child. In the discipline of the mind, the past is, all-important.

Here was an outsider. Here was an Englishman who was well educated, articulate and apparently leading a band in the jazz capital of America, and a man utterly at home with music born out of slavery and suffering. What is the relationship between jazz, suffering and Chaucer's musical talent? What was Chaucer's original interest in jazz?

"Jazz; let me see; jazz; or music in general? No; it must be jazz."

Chaucer looked at Surette quizzically.

"The answer should be obvious. Without regard to the colour of your skin, which suggests your heritage and bloodlines are related to the pioneers, you have been around jazz your whole life. There must be very little I can teach you or indeed explain to you. What is on your doorstep should be obvious, unless its proximity blinds you."

Surette considered the proposition that skin and heritage made him suited to understanding New Orleans' most profitable export. But he didn't understand jazz. He didn't understand the relevance of his skin either.

"Presumably you have a sense of rhythm; a feeling for sound; a faculty for the gaps and holes within the rationale of sound; a need to invent sound around what is commonly expected?"

Peripheral; Surette wanted to know why Chaucer liked jazz. What had fired the Englishman's interest?

"Easy. There was a boy, say a teenager, who bandaged and wrapped creativity and pain around the fundamentals of his character; indeed, each fed upon and regenerated the other, for many reasons. But what he also had, although for the first seventeen years of his life he wasn't aware of the alternative outlet, was the innate ability to let these qualitatively different features of his essence, resolve and educate his mind.

Clarity; you will have guessed who that teenager was. I was a little ball of creation and pain, intertwined. And one day, when the virulous temptations looting the insides of my head caused me to think that my star could get no lower, I picked up a trumpet. A trumpet. Sounds asinine doesn't it? It is asinine. A trumpet.

Silly instrument; silly sound - can sound like an elephant; can sound like the stuff of Gods - depends; still, the trumpet. Not the sort of device one associates with saving a young life. Not that the trumpet was my saviour alone I must add, but enough of a conduit to give me a voice; something through which I could express those feelings which used to take me in all of the wrong directions; to help me direct my inner leanings away from insanity and the manifestations of madness. I woke up and found out what my ears were for. I found out that of all the things I could have done and have done, the one thing I am made to do involves a little brass pipe and my own way of assembling the fifteen notes within an octave. That is simply said of course as jazz still involves all of the intellectual stamina one can muster, and all of the mathematics a small mind like mine can deal with. Jazz is such a wonderful discipline, with intellectual force living alongside the dialect of pain neighbouring the natural talent to put it together and make what comes out of my trumpet mean something to me and to others who want to listen.

Well, words are not exactly my strong point, Doctor. Words are what everybody else uses and I am still rather eloquent. Taking away music would finish me off."

Strange how Chaucer had and hadn't answered the question, with music being some sort of release and escape mechanism for him to use during the emotional turbulence of his early years. Still he had nothing of why those years were turbulent and nothing precise in relation to the reason why jazz in particular, suited Will Chaucer's needs.

"Don't you see, Doctor? For jazz to work as an art form, one needs pain, wherever that pain comes from. Maybe it lies in centuries of subjugation - the subjugation of the Afro-American community here, or the pain that coloured my early years. Discovering this music was the key to an understanding that extended far beyond my own experience. Jazz allowed me to tap into an organisation developed out of suffering. Collective suffering brought jazz itself to life and playing the trumpet brought me closer to collective suffering and man's answer to it."

Chaucer sounded conclusive, advocating that jazz itself was, in a sense, irrelevant - a means to an end and confirmation that the spirit and the injustices of a past life could be assuaged through sound. Surette doubted it. His profession was concerned with the analysis of the human condition using and developing ideas through the one common currency amongst all peoples - language.

"Of course it is arguable that there are many mediums of language, be it sign language or the stretch of the vocal chords conveying the mind. Each is an agency of sound, equivocal with music. Believe me Doctor; language bears no relationship to music."

Surette found the comment confusing.

"Listen; language itself is about the articulation of understanding. It could be said that music is the same. Yet you have to answer this question - if music were the same as the word or whatever other communicative medium you care to mention, then why aren't we all musicians? Why did I find recompense for the turbulence of my childhood in my ability to invent answers through jazz?

The ability to produce sound beyond the very mortal capacities of language is in the way the brain works quite apart from the brain's base qualities. You can't think your way into being a musician. And if you can't think your way into being a musician, you certainly can't improvise.

The ability to interpret the world of sound lies in the innate construction of the brain. Sound comes from within. Talent, let me be commonplace, is rather more of a gift than a right.

What turns the musician into the musician who improvises over the rules of sound is more and less than that. It is also the accumulation of experience. It is about sensitivity to pain. Jazz is the expression of pain and pleasure which, in my opinion, is unique; consider - genetic capacity; generations of repression - not exactly a unique combination but a combination all the same which has given America some of the greatest ambassadors of musical thought."

Vague supposition - Chaucer had to equate supposition with practise.

"I have had rather a rough life. I have the innate ability to express that upbringing in a way that is both meaningful to me and meaningful to the people who pay money to listen. But there is one more thing - a matter which is almost impossible to express in language. In fact the English language is ill equipped to express it at all. Even the Greek language, articulated as it was by ancient philosophers who first came across the experience, complained that ancient Greek was an insufficient medium of communication to express music's superior quality."

Surette was lost.

"The human quality I am referring to is astonishment."

Inadequacy was not a feeling Roux Surette was used to. His forte was control - control of his environment no matter what that environment entailed. Chaucer was taking him somewhere he had never been before, unless Chaucer was deliberately trying to confuse him.

"Believe me the correct emotion is astonishment - not the kind that fills a child's face when it first sees a tiger, or a lion; no - astonishment lies in improvisation, which is the cornerstone of jazz and the bedrock upon which the medium derives its distinguished identity.

What constantly astonishes is the way jazz unveils the inner man emanating from the intimate gyrations of melodious schemes, and asks questions without obvious answers. It is of the moment and the moment allows forth a passageway for the correct brain to express in almost perfect sympathy the connections between experience and expression. Language for all its inestimable qualities cannot do this. Language is not qualified to do this.

For this reason, the appropriate way to describe what it is I hear but can't control when I start to convey my feelings along and down the brass tube that makes up my particular instrument, is astonishment.

Do you understand?

I am indeed, a privileged man. I can put forward ideas through a combination of ability and experience denied to the majority of the population and, I can pacify the deleterious experiences which marked my early years."

Evidently there was, according to Chaucer's analysis, a close relationship between trauma, music and release. But if one didn't have the mechanics of release, or what Chaucer had called innate ability, then the whole process would be meaningless. Music would be meaningless. And it was at least a basic truism that not all who enjoyed music had that gift.

Surette wanted to pursue another point relevant to the death of Darius Trémé. Surette anticipated that it lay in the concept of release. He wondered whether Chaucer was making that very point.

"Well; yes. See I am able to let go of my past in a way that is beneficial to me and to the community. What happens Doctor, if one has an environment and an individual within that environment who doesn't have the means, exterior or interior, to release the angst of the past in a fruitful and accommodatory way?

The matter is clear enough. Whoever killed that boy, Darius Trémé, has, and excuse me if I get a little romantic in my language here, suffered horribly at the hands of an individual, community or society, within which that individual still resides. The killer, be it an man, which is what we almost expect, or a woman, which is what we do not expect, is someone who has had to contend and live with the most violent and hideous trauma for many, many years. Perhaps they live in apparent happiness. It is even conceivable that the person responsible for mutilating that little appears to be a bastion of responsibility and care. Yet what is apparent is an individual who has reached the limit of their tolerance.

A particular event may have caused the change. An external source has unloaded and brought to shore the violence of the past. And now that delivery has taken place and the killer has breached for the first time the hideousness of capability, it is, as I told you, only a matter of time before someone else dies.

What would I do if I couldn't play the trumpet? I couldn't improvise? I couldn't exude the astonishment my make-up is capable of creating through sound? I couldn't help myself in the way I can assist in the imagination of others? I couldn't give pleasure to others yet giving that pleasure and assisting myself was something I wanted? What else would I do? What would you do if you discovered self-help in the sustenance of murder; mutilation; of killing someone as innocent as a seven-year-old boy; of trying to leave a trail of clues and source material for your particular brand of angst; finding self-help in eviscerating others? You would keep doing it. You would not stop. Originally you asked why jazz? Jazz is therapy to me; jazz and blues was therapy for the pain of the masses - therapy for me, of benefit to the masses. Change the question. Why kill a child? Why mutilate a child? Torture a child? Eviscerate a child?

The answer?

Therapy."

With Roux Surette lost in thought, Quinn came into Surette's study and passed him a hand delivered letter adorned with the crest of the New Orleans Police Department.

The message was simple and precise....

"Surette; liaise with this officer - his name is Olivier Godin. He will be in touch shortly."

The letter was signed, "Eveny Brien."

IX.

"He is a relatively uninteresting character for New Orleans. His ordinariness is what makes him successful. Plenty have used his services, although they wouldn't dare admit it. He is calm and measured and exudes intelligence. But I must say, even though I am an acquaintance, Surette would be the first to admit that a lot of his job is simply sitting and listening while patients unveil. He finds little of interest in a lot of them and often doesn't listen. His ordinariness is what makes him easy to speak to. Whatever quirks he has, he keeps them well hidden.

But he has done something to upset someone very senior in the New Orleans political fraternity. I am not at liberty to say who it is. The call was made last night shortly after the remains of Darius Trémé were found. Someone has thought about this very carefully. It is self-evident that Roux Surette is no Detective and putting this kind of pressure upon the man was a deliberate act. He is simply a psychiatrist. His relationship with the New Orleans police department is symbolic at best. I don't think, when he agreed a few years ago to be our adviser, that he envisaged being involved. But involved he is. And whoever made the choice to put the Trémé killer upon his head started with a phone call to this office and another to the press. Ideally, they should not have known about his involvement. Roux Surette's job is now significantly harder. Whether he realises it or not, he is the public fall guy should this killer strike again. You, of course, will suffer in isolation.

I will protect you and so allow you to get on with your job. You can do this with anonymity but the rate of acceleration should you fail, will be severe. Surette may go down outside - you will descend here, unseen and unheard.

Do you have any leads Godin?"

Godin's response was basic, deciding that there was no reason to try and sound convincing - three hours into the investigation and he had nothing convincing to say.

"So Surette is with another patient and isn't available?"

Godin sensed Brien's surprise.

"This must be a remarkable individual to keep Surette away from the task in hand. Try him again and do not take no for an answer. His wife says he has no sense of perspective. He will search and dwell on answers so that time and circumstance have no meaning. I expect you to wake him from this slumber and drag him toward this case. Surette will provide you with a tick-list of type and it is up to you to put the type to the masses and come up with the killer. The pathology of this particular killer is as unique as it is disturbing. Past files and types would be unlikely to give you even the tiniest of assistance. The key to the particular lies in estimations of manner and past - something in the past of the killer unveiling clues. I sincerely hope for the sake of your career that Surette's estimations of manner add up to more than his manners so far."

Godin wasn't listening. Her words weren't hollow, nor were they lost, as his thought processes sifted through the consequences of her words. He was trying to establish how to respond and to do that, he was attempting to get a definitive impression of what lay beyond her words and the directions of her sympathies, should she have any. This was a somewhat unusual situation. Normally he kept to himself, letting his work speak for him. The lesson was learnt very early in his career, for no one had ever trusted him or given him the benefit of the doubt. He had grown weary and defensive over the years and concluded that silence and control were the only effective shields he had when nobody wanted to help. But here was a woman intimating that she was on his side. He wondered whether he could trust her. But there was too much ambiguity. When she offered protection, she did so proffering disaster. When she offered support, she credited him with the benefit of failure. He didn't want to expose his inner thoughts as if he was an onion and she was peeling just so many layers away. He had learnt the hard way that a soft, thoughtful, or an unsure centre, gave the opposition power; an advantage; an angle to punish. He wasn't ready to put even the tips of his fingers above the trench. The body has two temperatures - an inner and an outer flux. While the temperature of the outer can fluctuate wildly and the inner will survive, expose the inner to the elements and slight fluctuations will cause the body to die. He would keep his counsel.

Once again, he tried to contact Surette. He had now tried on six separate occasions to speak to the psychiatrist. While Surette's secretary was polite, she was polite and firm - Surette was with a patient and wouldn't be seeing or speaking to anybody until he had finished. Godin wondered about Brien's words - that this patient must be a remarkable individual to keep Surette away from the task in hand.

Surette's clinic was a two hundred-yard, four-block walk, straight down Royal Street. When Godin got closer, he noticed the press camped outside Surette's door and worried parents outside the gates of the school opposite.

Noting that there was one entrance and one exit from Surette's building, Godin slipped into the community coffee shop opposite, on the corner of Royal and St Philippe, ordered tea and sat down. He looked at his watch. It was coming up to lunchtime. If there was going to be any movement from within Surette's clinic, maybe lunchtime would be it. Godin kept himself focused on Roux Surette's door.

As his mind started to wander, Godin looked up just as a man with black hair appeared from Surette's clinic and slipped through the barriers erected to keep back the press. A hunch – intuition; Godin gambled that the unknown male he was following was the object of Surette's interest.

The male with black hair walked up Royal Street, slowly and deliberately, without suspicion, neither unfazed nor distracted by the street performers, drunks and show-offs scratching for a few dollars on the street, walking four blocks north and turning right. Watching closely, Godin saw nothing odd in the way he traversed the streets save for one thing - each time he came to cross the road, he instinctively looked to the right, whether or not the cars on The French Quarter's one-way streets came from the right or not. It was as if he expected traffic to move from the right. An American man crossing the road instinctively looks to the left. He, looked the opposite way. Simple reasoning suggested that the man Godin was following was not an American and was likely to be a Brit, where they drive on the left hand side of the road.

Eventually, he took a right on to Toulouse. After a couple of blocks he turned left onto Bourbon Street then took in a long stretch to the top of Bourbon where Godin watched him step into Whites. Convinced he had gone unnoticed, Olivier Godin did the same.

Godin ordered a drink. Godin noticed him immediately, standing on Whites' stage. He produced a battered trumpet from his instrument case. The case remained open and he blew a few notes. He was good, Godin thought - excellent in fact, and pre-occupied. While this trumpeter was playing be-bop riffs, periodically disappearing behind a curtain, Godin slipped quietly to the side of the stage and looked at the address on the inside of his instrument case. Thirty seconds later and Godin had left Whites with a name and an address - Will Chaucer, Jericho, Oxford, England.

Godin decided to establish the circumstances of Will Chaucer's entry into the US. Chaucer had arrived from London Heathrow eleven or so months previously with a twelve-month work permit. Godin tried to see if there was any record of criminality in the United States - petty crime; a scuffle in a bar; urinating in a public place; a little too much to drink. Nothing. He tried another tack, calling Whites and speaking to the manager. How long would Will Chaucer and his band be staying and if not, where they were booked to play next?

Tomorrow was Chaucer's last night at Whites. The manager wasn't aware that the band had any more engagements in the New Orleans area, the reason not being a lack of offers as the band was by all accounts, brilliant; for his own reasons, Will Chaucer wanted to leave New Orleans.

Godin cursed for not making the connection earlier. Chaucer's visa was about to run out. He had to leave the Unites States the day after next. Godin checked the man's status with the airlines. Chaucer's booking had been confirmed. A child is murdered and a suspect is booked to leave the country after the fact but not too quickly. If this Englishman had killed Darius Trémé, then why kill the boy a couple of days before he was to leave? Why not do it just before his flight departed?

Godin remembered meeting an English police officer at a conference in New Orleans, a few years earlier. Tom Byron had been seconded to New Orleans as part of a US law enforcement awareness programme. Godin still had his card somewhere. Byron was a decorated Detective based in Scotland Yard and had worked some of the more horrific murders in London.

Though it was late in London, Godin was in luck, apologised and enquired about the possibility of conducting a records search through Scotland Yard's criminal archives against the name of William Xavier Chaucer, and an address, namely, 33 Great Clarendon Street, Jericho, Oxford.

Tom Byron should have refused the request. But the quid pro quo nature of US-UK relations allowed Byron to circumvent procedure. However, as Byron explained, a comprehensive résumé was going to take at least a few hours and results wouldn't probably be known until the next afternoon English time - the next morning in New Orleans. Godin thanked his English colleague profusely and bit his lip. If he had to wait until the morning, then he would just have to wait.

X.

Chaucer sat almost motionless, his eyes flitting between Surette and the further distances he seemed to need. Surette was impressed. It wasn't that Chaucer was smart - every dotard lawyer, banker, doctor or accountant could lay claim to that particular epitaph; no; Chaucer's was a perception beyond the normality arising from the constituent parts of achievement, with the ability to grasp what was within the shell around which motivation and the drive for success emanated; an advanced idea of the lesser proclivities of man; of suffering, which Chaucer claimed was through his own suffering; and an interesting idea of how to alleviate suffering through the auspices of his talent for music, in particular, jazz - and, that strange and seemingly nonsensical reference to the idea of astonishment.

Astonishment seemed to arise when Chaucer improvised during performance, relying on his ear's relationship with the surrounding chord structure, with limited control over the way his mind interpreted its environment. Then how, constantly, he was astonished at his use of the chords and freedom jazz offered, releasing him from the hideousness of his early years.

"Perhaps a note - just a note, placed somewhere in the structure where it does the most damage and thus becomes the most creative force."

And the ability to appreciate the surprise inherent in his own improvisations; as if he went on to automatic pilot during performance; a man capable of improvised understanding from several perspectives - that which came from analysis and an appreciation of the environment, juxtaposed by a rounded erudition and innate intelligence, and a further reality which Surette did not have and did not need - of conveyance and exculpation from within; through sound; through the medium of jazz.

So what had happened in his early life that led Chaucer to the darker corners from where he had claimed escape?

"I have your word that our quid pro quo arrangement exists? Should I tell you of the circumstances which led me to New Orleans, you will guarantee that my profile will get to the right people?"

Surette was smug; for having been bowled over by the eloquence and charisma of the Englishman, the tables had turned.

"Sensing that I have debilitations and disturbances; watching my demeanour change and my veil coming down, isn't going to give your arrogant potentialities some scope. You are not going to have the upper hand when I declare the contours of my palm. That would get in the way of your clinical judgement, would it not?

Where to start; we have so little time. It started at school; a special school; a school for the gifted. But first there was ordinariness.

Life at home was a very poor, once industrial enclave in middle England; a puritanical background - motivations to work through the fear of failure and hard work being an absolute. I attended two schools - the first is in my home town and a very religious, puritanical college with strict and rather perverse values; the second was a boarding school with attendance on the basis of aptitude for music."

I attended the second school when I was thirteen years old. Two months to the day after my thirteenth birthday I won a scholarship to attend a boarding school for musically gifted children, about sixty miles away from home, meaning that I had to leave home for the majority of the year, for five years.

This was home for children from all over the world - the most expensive boarding school in Europe; the most privileged children in Europe - more pianos than pupils; more practise rooms than pupils; more professors attending upon children and their needs than any of the major music colleges in England. There was I, poor and insular, with an accent and psychology ill-suited to the world I had chosen to inhabit - poverty of means and poverty of perspective, pushed into peoples who were the opposite."

Surette considered the connections with music and a child unable to converse and understand. The logic of that situation would be the search for solace in a known medium - the solace of sound; the solace, of music.

"I was enamoured with my new environment at first, and in some ways it was an easy world; in others, not so easy. You see the person who arrived at music school those years ago, was incredibly ill, with a mind that deserved hours upon a psychiatrist's couch, and probably still does.

I was, musical. And music became my life. Music afforded me the opportunity for escape; to grow and breach the span from dysfunctional child to barely functional adult. Yes; I had many demons to confront; my upbringing was fraught; and my behaviour, complex. But music and music school was good for me. The emancipation gave me one more perspective; and I could yet make further sense of my appalling past."

Chaucer's family - it had to be; and Surette had to ask.

"It is to do with my stepmother. It happened years before."

Chaucer took in a breath; he took an age to exhale. For the first time, Surette felt close; closer to the man; closer to the truth.

"My first memories were being taught to hit, Doctor - to strike; to lash out; to pummel and destroy with my fists what my mind was told not to handle; to do everything except kill. It is a difficult thing to explain to a four-year-old boy that trying to maim and injure other children is the appropriate way to behave - crying was wrong; complaining was wrong; courage was right - physical courage, of course. The more people I attacked the better a stepson I was. And if I wanted something, I took it. If that meant hurting others with my fists, sticks, or whatever other implements I had to hand, then so be it. There were no rules out in the street on which I lived, nor should I have expected there to be any rules - kick, gouge, bite, scratch, stab, and scar - no rules.

The only time law was enforced was when I failed. Physical punishment began at home. Beatings would be endless with fear the motivating force behind all action - fail and be punished; punished with the raw end of a boot; punished with a fist or quite simply being thrown into doors and walls. It didn't matter; it all hurt and it all had to be avoided. Hurt other people because they would try to hurt you - a hideous disregard for the mind of a child - my mind. In fact, no concern for my mind, save to fill it full of hatred; to assume the worst of everyone; to expect the worst of myself.

The outcome was an infusion of hatred into the mind of a four-year-old who became a hate-filled five-year-old and a vile six-year-old. Truly, every inclination I was taught lied at the bottom of a trough of morality and at the evil end of a continuum from good to insidious. By deed, I was an evil boy. I inflicted pain on everything. I assumed everything would inflict pain upon me. And if I failed to inflict pain, pain was inflicted upon me."

Distance; distance - Chaucer seemed far removed from the child he said he was. Psychiatric theory establishes that the defining characteristics of personality are infused within the first six years of life. Violence could be one of them. Hatred could be one of them too and regardless of subsequent development, these basic instincts remained within the individual and the individual would find them impossible to disregard. You are what you are, is an oft-quoted phrase - a cliché, like most clichés, it exhibits a fundamental truth.

The question remained. How did this rather gentle looking man with rather sad eyes; how did the rather gentle looking man mutate from the monster he had described into what he appeared to be?

"The urges and proclivities are still within. I constructed a way out. The de-construction of the innate however, was by no means the end of the matter. It was a beginning.

One day, when I was nine, I was playing soccer in the schoolyard. I was, by this time about nine years of age. By that time I had developed a track history of bullying and administering pain; but aligned with the kind of effort that took me to the top of my class in every subject - mathematics, English, art, sport. You name it I fought and fought to win; and won - an ego developed; a sense of indestructibility.

I was playing soccer and I lost the ball, which was taken off me by someone who took it upon himself to make a point and laugh at me. Enraged, I waited until the protagonist was at his weakest and, like a true coward, hit him with such force that he ended up in hospital. Not that I could care much at the time as ending up in hospital was a good day's work for me. Putting him into a hospital - hospitalising him, was a good day's work.

No; the thing was, at the moment when I struck that boy, every single person in my class, boy or girl, chased and tracked, hunted and sought me out with one intention in mind - to kill. Nine year old children hunting in a pack to try and maim the person sitting before you with the weapons they had brought to hand, Doctor; kids who had turned wild; kids who had become feral; kids who had grown tired of my personality; my urge to use violence; the bullying; the physical and psychological pain. For four years they had put up with what I had done to them while I thought nothing of what I was doing.

And for about thirty minutes they chased me until I was out of breath, adrenalin pushing me further and further away and fear carrying my system for the very first time. But they didn't catch me. Too clever by half I was able to double back. Straight back into school I ran, back through the school gates, back into the classroom, back into the room where safety resided. I ran straight into the arms of my stepmother. And my stepmother pushed me straight back into the arms of the mob."

Slowly and deliberately, Chaucer stood up and removed his shirt, showing Surette his chest and his arms, then his back. Chaucer's torso was riddled with scars, teeth marks and scratch marks - twisted skin cut, flayed and mangled, ripped and torn apart. Not a section of Will Chaucer's torso was left untouched; not a piece of flesh on his arms or on his back.

"I could show you my legs if you want. It isn't necessary. I spent two weeks in hospital and three months off school; numerous skin grafts thereafter; the longest three and a half months of my life; the worst three and a half months of my life; and the most important three and a half months of my life. You see Doctor; I was put in a bed next to the boy I had hit in the schoolyard."

Chaucer looked down, blinked slowly and protruded his bottom lip.

"I had fractured his skull."

Connections; and intimate parts of this man's tapestry were beginning to make sense - the walk from child to adult littered with events Chaucer saw as significant and important to his development as a person; Will Chaucer describing his past as if he was an outsider; had become an outsider; a man looking in on himself as if he were a different person altogether, watching his actions and learning how to deal with idiosyncrasies he now believed were the immoral characteristics of a child, knowing that the way he had acted was based upon instincts he had begun to understand only after the shock of his own despisement.

It wasn't so much that the boy I lay next to was someone I had noticed before. He was quiet and sensitive and I had never needed to compete with him. His was a different outlook - one of moderation and thought for others. And the crucial question when I woke up in hospital, looking at him, watching his puzzled face, or that portion of his face which wasn't obscured by bandages and tubes, was the question which changed the course of my life - why?

Why? And I couldn't answer. I didn't know why I had hit him. Why was not a question I understood. To do was all. To question anything other than the need to win and hurt was anathema to me."

Surette thought of Chaucer's stepmother.

"Well; that is the point. Watching that boy's face formulate the question, bemused perhaps but filled with a deep lack of understanding and curiosity as to why I had hurt him so badly, filled me with a deep and hitherto unknown sense of guilt. Precisely where that feeling of shame came from, that sense of guilt, I do not know. It is a question I have asked myself many times.

I have subsequently decided that the answer isn't one to be known conclusively - maybe from my environment; from within perhaps - an innate sense of what is right and wrong. To provide a conclusive answer to that problem would provide the world at large with a finite response to one of the great philosophical debates and I do not myself, pretend to know from where the myriad of wells the human spirit springs from. But an infinite variety of wellsprings are there.

The appearance of guilt and a deep lack of understanding in the course of that day - the day I started with an endless self-examination, has helped me to assert a moral purpose and outcome in relation the machinations of my own personality. And those months off school, tending my wounds, beginning to establish the reasons why I was the way I was, made in small part, the man you see before you and led me down a road of pain and suffering I would not wish on another human being on earth."

Chaucer's stepmother - it was obvious.

"Yes; my stepmother. Let me tell you what she did to me. Let me tell you what I did to her. The beatings did not stop. They continued. There was no remorse for pushing me outside and into the arms of the mob; with claims from her that I had let myself down; that I had not fought back enough as the mob tore me apart; claims of disappointment and a degree of remorse on her part that the virus she had planted within, had not gestated effectively - that I wasn't the son she wanted; that I was a weak and ineffective performer on the psychotic stage.

So she grew worse; and frustrated. And for the first time, as I looked down upon my scarred body, which reminded me constantly of all that had been done to me, I began to question her and fight back; and counter every inflection in her voice and every immoral purpose she extolled upon me with an answer of my own.

The question always why - why hurt? They will hurt you otherwise. Why violence? Do unto them as they will do unto you. Why make others suffer? For you will suffer more if you don't - twisted logic Doctor - twisted and undeniably evil, logic.

I read too; I read widely - to search for sophisticated answers with which to put her down; matters getting worse as I did so; her only answer to an erudite boy - fists, knees, brute strength against my weak, childish frame. Truly, it was hideous and it went of for years; from the age of nine onwards; all the time me developing responses to the insidious urges which still, to this day, reside within my mind - patterns of thought a constant battle between urge and examination of that very same urge. Sure I wanted to hurt people but I put all of my energy into learning control.

Now do you see the point; the reason why I am here? The reason why I announced my presence here by declaring you inadequate for the task of profiling the killer of Darius Trémé?

With my utmost apologies, I felt it necessary to make an entrance of sorts and to give you a little food for thought as to why an Englishman should invade your good offices and offer you this apparently unqualified service. As you see, I am not unqualified in the language of violence, or what causes it, or the best way to deal with it. Regardless of formal qualification Doctor, do you see how I am qualified to assist and guide in a way you cannot, given that you are just a soothsayer in the environment of the mind? You are, in fact, barely qualified to understand the myriad of ways of individual expression, in whatever context you care to imagine. Ultimately you are indebted to the very people who understand the psychology of madness because they have thought through it and are able to clarify madness itself - deep-rooted madness; the sort of madness that only those privy to the world in which madness unveils itself, can understand - world of urge and counter-reason; the playground of the intelligent; the playground a juxtaposition between sanity and the cavernous environs labelled insanity.

Only through my understanding, I feel, can we both deal with whatever stalks the French Quarter in New Orleans and attend to the needs of the killer at the same time."

Arrogance - still Surette sensed arrogance; yet Surette had to contend with Chaucer's reasoning and put matters into context. He was now in a corner. The New Orleans police department had passed the buck. The press were involved. The Orlean community had given him an ultimatum. Darius Trémé's killer would kill again. With another death, the pressure would be intense. Details of how Darius Trémé was killed were already in the press; moral panic; questions; Surette inexperienced in this sort of thing, needing, if his ego let him absorb the need, someone's assistance.

Could Will Chaucer help? He seemed adamant he was going to. He seemed to have a good case, as he unveiled the kind of psychological superstructure designed to avoid all of the vagaries of what happened to be a hideously maladjusted upbringing.

Surette knew he had little to lose. Will Chaucer was already part of the tapestry of the case, though Surette still had many questions to ask. Personality characteristics are composed of competing and often counter-balancing voices, or a conflict of mediating forces. Interesting in Chaucer's case, was the base severity of the urges to punish and hurt; and the corresponding severity of his mechanics of control with respect to those very urges. This gave Chaucer an extremely strong mental apparatus. It also gave him the potential for far-reaching and distorting side effects, which Chaucer claimed were alleviated through the medium of sound. The comparison between self-help through jazz therapy, and the therapy of ritualistic murder, was a good reflection upon the mind of the killer where something had gone wrong; where something had mutated and reformed.

"You haven't asked me about my father. My relationship with my father was more often than not tainted by my father's relationship with my stepmother. As you may well imagine, if a child starts to contradict and counter a violent bully, then one has a cocktail wherein my father more often than not, had to choose between the protestations and violence of my stepmother and the counter-acting passivity I chose as the best way of nullifying her teaching.

More often than not my father sided with me. My stepmother saw this as an expression of disloyalty and consequently, began to use violence against my father too.

Interesting; often I notice people finding violence funny. Violence is endemic in practically all cultures but more often than not, our sense of humour is built around people getting hurt, be it slapstick or the kinds of stories one hears in across a crowded or, indeed, an empty bar.

The actuality of violence is so ugly - so ugly, that I can understand humour coming out as a way of dealing with it, but the physicality of violence itself is so ugly that simple words cannot do the concept justice. I can tell you that my stepmother began hitting and humiliating my father, but your imagination cannot readily appreciate in all its actual detail the montage of blood, screaming, anger, bitterness, denial, pleading and destruction that took place in the name of my non-acceptance of the language of the thug."

Did he feel guilt?

"Of course I felt guilt. There isn't a day goes by when I think of how I could have done things differently; how I could have forgotten the selfishness of my own self-induced mission to alleviate my violent propensities in order to save my father from the unhappiness of the life which grew around him. I could see no other way. And I could not anticipate on the day I countered the essence of my personality, that the ramifications for my father would be catastrophic. They may well have been catastrophic for him anyway. It was only a matter of time before my stepmother got to work on him. Still, that doesn't matter now."

Surette asked why.

"My stepmother is dead, apparently, although she is officially still classified as a missing person."

Remorse?

"Good God; no. If I could only use words as vehicles to infuse you with the hatred and contempt I still feel for every atom of that woman's body, wherever that body may be, then you would be just about on the verge of understanding all that that man put me through and all that man created, when she attempted to create me."

Interesting; Chaucer admitted that he loathed himself; that he looked deep within and found only the most detestable qualities.

"Well, on that point Doctor, you are entirely correct. But what am I supposed to do? I am trapped by the urges given to me before I was in a position to reject those very same urges. Under nurture, I have violence stamped all over me. With control, I have an element of sanity. With music; with jazz; I have release."

Surette thought of himself for a moment. He had never examined the idiosyncrasies of his own personality in the way that Chaucer had examined his. It was as if Chaucer had looked deep within to find the origin of all meaning.

"Yes; why everything - sick but addictive Doctor - why do I smile when I don't feel like smiling; why do I laugh when I don't find matters funny; why should I talk when I don't feel like talking; why do, anything? What motivates at all? What is the origin of the person in the annals of meaning? What am I and how can I change it?"

There is no right to happiness. I am an honest man. Happiness does not grow in honesty. Happiness is the language of compromise. Anyway; I am digressing again - I will loathe my stepmother until I die. I love my father."

Surette returned to the question of violence. He wanted to know if the Chinese walls Chaucer had erected within had ever been breached.

"If you are asking me whether I have ever hurt another person with my fists since the day I was mutilated, the answer is no. But if you were to ask whether I had thought about it since I was a child, then the answer is yes, often in situations that seem to have no relation to my past. I have even dreamed of it. The urge is still inside me, and it is inside the person who killed Darius Trémé."

Surette asked he envisaged a situation when he could be violent, again.

"No. No; no."

Surette sensed a man skipping over into territory he did not want to go. When Surette made the point, Chaucer was calm and reasoned.

"No. I will confirm to you now, I will never indulge in the violence of my past, in the future. The language of violence is abhorrence itself. I will not let it steal from me any more."

Surette took stock. He had Chaucer's early years; he had Chaucer's music. He had elements of the way in which Will Chaucer ticked inside and somewhat of an Achilles heal. But there still seemed as if there was something missing. Surette wondered if Chaucer had developed relationships. He wondered if anybody had been close to him. Roux Surette wondered what kind of a person could get close to him.

XI.

Godin understood the blood-rhyme for its simplicity; its banality -
a commonly held hateful residue of the horrors of man. Godin looked at the
blood-rhyme and saw himself. Godin looked up and saw hatred in the eyes
of his men outside. The blood rhyme spoke; and so did the venal faces of
these detractors staring at him. Blood was on the killer's hands; blood, too,
was on the minds of the hate squad who despised him for the breaching the
norm and being different.

Where did these mutations of decency and honesty came from? He
was not diseased; he was not abnormal. He was decent; he was kind.
Sometimes, he was lonely and wanted to belong. But he had no friends; he
had no partner. Godin had no other voice save for his own, and the only
time he articulated his concerns was with his mute father.

These twisted, dislocated words of a killer spoke of isolation and
repression; and isolation and repression by their very nature needed an

outlet for the purveyor. This man had chosen to kill a child. What had he, Olivier Godin, chosen?

Derision, loneliness and rejection seemed such a high price to pay for the tainted gift of unknown origin that made his eyes seek out the same sex. The job of catching the killer had forced their hand; and Godin was sensing the needs of the crowd. His denouement would be the crystallization of their justice and the pressure would be brought to bear.

The actions of the killer and the minutiae of the rhyme evoked a mindset that had snapped - pressure; intense pressure as its fulcrum; a mindset repressing then releasing controlling urges and releasing bitterness by emasculating innocence. The blood rhyme detailed a man who had examined the environment and castigated the good luck of others. Hatred directed action and fused wickedness, bitterness, jealousy, destruction and desire. The killer seemed to be explaining how the destruction of innocence was worthy of applause.

Godin sympathised, as humanity had turned out to be inhumanity; and he too would suffer at the hands of man. Yet what defined him would be his differences from the killer; and his differences from the hate squad. Pride and decency gave him strength. He only wished that the killer had shown the same degree of fortitude.

"Do not stand up. Please; spare me the formality."

As she smiled, Godin sensed sincerity. He assumed the opposite.

"I can't see where we are going with that stupid text. One could look at it all day and see a million different things. One could even see oneself. There are bits of everybody in those words if you look hard enough. Its general nature loses it validity."

Godin returned her words with a smile. Indeed; she was perceptive. Undoubtedly, he was in that rhyme. He had more in common with the killer than most.

"The phone log has you making a call to Scotland Yard. You have asked for a profile of a William Xavier Chaucer - an English musician in New Orleans, and presumably the patient Surette seems to be enamoured with. May I ask why?"

Godin explained his suspicions - the plane ticket; the timing of his appearance; the difficulty in seeing Surette. He explained how he was being speculative; intuitive. With no other leads, what did he have to lose?

"And Scotland Yard will not be able to get back until tomorrow afternoon at the earliest?"

Godin confirmed.

"And you have nothing from forensics; you have the French Quarter guarded with all of the manpower at our disposal; you have the French Quarter's schoolchildren safely looked after by their teachers and thereafter their parents? So you are at a loss for a while until something happens; Surette gets back to you; Scotland Yard gets back to you?

Then get your jacket. There is little else you can do for now. I'm afraid I have some rather bad news. Your father has been taken ill. He has been ambulanced to hospital. I am afraid that he has suffered a stroke, albeit that his condition has been described as stable."

Unconcerned with the empty and unknowing stares outside, Godin fled his room to the basement car park where Eveny Brien's Mercedes waited. His hands were sweating; he felt weak. He felt nauseous too, as if his stomach was lined with weed killer.

"Your father has a private room. You can spend as long as you need to."

Brien put the car into drive. Godin wondered why Brien was coming with him. Of course, Brien knew who his father was.

"Jack Godin was a great Detective. He was a fine man. There is a lot of him in you. Integrity is hard to come by in public service and it doesn't lend itself to ingratiation. It takes a brave man to counter the immorality of the force, with its skewed rules and understandings. You have lasted so far; I wonder how far you are prepared to go. Keeping yourself chained up only adds petrol to their fire. Should you solve this murder I am willing to let you have the space you need. But you need to solve this case and you need to consider the value of proclaiming what you are. This social dismissal; you can't change them unless you are willing to win their respect with your bravery."

Few of Brien's words sunk in. Godin was assuming the worst and suffering from flashbacks and disjointed reminiscences….he was a child on a paddleboat going up and down the Mississippi, looking down upon the swirling waters of the river below; he was a child looking from the window of an aircraft fascinated by the nonsensical movements of cars on the freeway, driving in many different directions; he was a spectator at a football match, watching the crowd leave as the game was over. He remembered looking at his left hand resting in his mother's palm; he looked to his right, where his right hand remained firmly enclosed in the safety of his father's enclosed hand. How happy he was then to watch in wonder at the myriad of ways in which the world turned. How different he felt now, as the world had closed around him and was trying stop him drawing breath.

Brien put her hand on his shoulder. Instinctively Godin pulled away.

"He was a strong man when I first met him. He will be a strong man, now."

Godin looked upon the palm that rested on his shoulder. If this was humanity, it was the first semblance of humanity he had received in years.

Jack Godin' room was located on the fourth floor of the New Orleans University Hospital. Godin had little time for nuance as he rushed up the stairs. As he walked into his father's room, he never noticed Eveny Brien close the door behind him and wait in the hall outside.

Godin looked down upon his father. He looked smaller. His legs were emaciated through lack of use, creeping back into his torso as if his torso were a protective shell. His neck looked thin and weak and the strong face had become lax and lifeless. A transparent tube was running fluids into his nose and another transparent tube was penetrating his forearm just above the wrist.

According to his nurse his condition was stable. How would they know? The man had no way of telling them how he felt. How would they be able to articulate his internal condition; his mental condition; how would they be able to ascertain his body's relationship with his mind? What, after all, did they understand about Parkinson's Disease?

The aching silence was occasionally broken by the electronic gurgle of a heart monitor. Godin held his father's hand. Grief was freezing his thoughts and without thought both father and son were mute. Fearing the worst, Godin could do no more than hang his head and let the enormity of the moment overwhelm him. He didn't want things to change; this was mealy and temporary; another day and another case to solve. His father had always helped him in the past; his father would help him now.

"She is outside, the new police chief I told you about. She drove me here and told me you were ill. I hope you can hear me. You have always heard me when no one else would listen."

Godin squeezed his father's hand. Jack Godin never moved. Godin kept looking at the steady beat of the heart monitor next to the bed, listening for monotony and the security of a steady beat.

"If ever I need you I need you now. I do not know what to do. The woman outside either wants my head or she wants to help me. You, father, are all I have. She has been kind to me but I worry she is being kind for motives I cannot construe. It is as I told you. Who has ever helped me as I try to serve people who need help? Why should I believe her now? All I can see is loss and gain from simple relationships. I do not want to get hurt. I do not want the indignity of pain anymore.

I have a suspect although I am not sure how strong a suspect he is. Circumstances lead me to the conclusion that he is involved - just intuition really, with no evidence. I am trying to profile him at the moment. I won't get any news until tomorrow. I am worried, father. The killer has the upper hand. We have no real leads and he is still out there. He can choose his moment and he can choose his place.

As for the rhyme left by the boy's body, it adds up to very little. The only person who is seemingly qualified to look at this more deeply is Roux Surette, but he is pre-occupied with the Englishman. And as I have come to expect, neither Surette nor anybody else wants to help me."

Godin looked over his shoulder. He thought he caught a glimpse of Eveny Brien.

"Brien seems to be the only one willing to assist. I do not trust her. How can I? It is like I told you so many times before. These people are not interested in catching the man who killed that boy. They would prefer to see another child die and allocate blame. All I want to do is help; all they want to do is to harm. I try not to feel sorry for myself. I try to help. But what have I to do to get them on my side? All I know is hatred, anger, bitterness and the vacuosity of these growing seeds of conjecture. I fear I will fail without your help. Please father; please."

Godin lent over the bed. A tear fell from his eye and fell into the pillow by his father's head. Godin kissed his father on the forehead. Then, as if trying to telepathically contact a dying man, he let their foreheads touch. Jack Godin didn't move. His body was still and lifeless. Momentarily, Olivier Godin' body lost all life too. Every sinew, molecule, every atom, every fleck of his soul and every tissue of his being wanted to infuse his father to tell him how much he loved him.

"I love you dad. Please. Don't go now. Don't leave me alone in this world. In this world you are all I have."

Life had left Olivier Godin - his will to live a trickle into dust. Godin knew nothing was worth pursuing anymore. Holding his father's hand, Olivier Godin had no thoughts left to give. He had no reason. He had no justifications to live and no one to express his feelings to.

"What is a man father if he cannot love? What is love if it cannot be attained? What is attainment if other men always defile you? What is attainment worth if one loses all? All is nothing when nothing is all. Life is dust and the elements control its direction. Truly I am lost. If I cannot be here father, take me with you, for I am dead already."

XII.

Surette was surprised at how easy it was to slide under Chaucer's skin. Chaucer was strong - strength arising out of the adverse; and adversity arising out of the awful minutiae of his past. It was a rare strength too - strength and intelligence; and a rare form of intelligence. The Englishman was a man unlike any he had ever listened to; a man who could commonly be passed as mentally unstable; a man in relation to whom a case could be made to have him interned and studied; yet a man advanced in so many ways. Surette was unaware of anyone in all the relevant literature exhibiting an equivalent psychological superstructure and understanding of the inner self. He was now convinced that Chaucer could have more than a positive impact in relation to profiling Darius Trémé's killer, though he felt that he was some distance from the heart of the man; and more than a head away from accepting his argument that experience is all.

If Chaucer was correct, then any man who had only known contentment was destined for diminished insight; and as Surette knew that he was contented, diminishment was his lot. Surette also recognised that Chaucer had an acuity that he wanted too; qualities he needed to have in order to get under the skin of all his clients. Currently, he was a fusion of theory and gleaned understanding. Chaucer's experience of violence and the mutations of personality violence can bestow upon a child, made Chaucer valuable in a way that the isolated experiences of a psychiatrist could not.

But what of Chaucer's relations - the same sex; the opposite sex; and the ages of enlightenment in any young man's life - Surette needed a touchstone, a lodestar, a guide; so Surette plumped for an old touchstone - relationships; love; sex.

"Why would you assume that I would skip anything you may consider crucial in your search for credibility?"

Surette wasn't quite sure he understood.

"That essence of me you crave stems not solely from my responses to violence or from my ability to offload violence through the medium of sound. There are other reasons why I am here. One of those reasons involves a relationship. And it just so happens that we met at school - music school."

Surette decided not to interject. Chaucer seemed morose, but a slight twinkle in his eye gave the impression that secretly, he enjoyed talking about a particular woman.

"She was the same age and played the violin. My first impression was one of distance - not physical distance but of a kind of separation from her surroundings as if, indeed, she was not part of the surroundings at all - an aura; an inviolable shield; but an inner vulnerability.

I say met - we made eye contact. There was something between us as our eyes pursued each other. Kindred spirits you may say."

Had Chaucer ever known a woman before?

"I had urges. Find me a seventeen-year-old male who isn't aware of his urges. Still; I did not have to go through the incremental growth patterns associated with teenage affairs of the heart. She was my one and only love."

Surette found that statement hard to believe. Here was a male, clearly an extremely attractive male, intimating that the flesh of other women had never tempted him. Chaucer was curt and dismissive.

"Should I have been? And if so; why?"

Surette was embarrassed. Daily frequencies of adulterers and short-term see-and-grab sexual terrorists had twisted his mind and so made cynical assumption the norm. It is bad practise for a psychiatrist to let cynicism overrule reason, even though his was a cynical bent richly deserved. Sexual-moral integrity wasn't really that prevalent in New Orleans, so images of sexual integrity weren't really that prevalent in Surette's mind. He asked how the relationship grew.

"Consider school; consider me. The other pupils spoke in good, formal English while I had an accent they could not understand. And these were students who understood nuances of social interaction I had never come across before. England has a culture within a culture within a culture. Each city, region, town and village has its own dialect, as do distinct areas of each city and each town. And each substratum has different if only slightly different mores as to right and wrong, good and bad. It is incredibly complicated - culture, mores, language; but not unique, I hasten to add. I may as well have come from outer space such were our differences. It is easy to see how one inverts and becomes insular."

Chaucer hadn't answered the question.

"I shut up, kept myself to myself and watched, learning to assimilate where necessary and were to withdraw if not. I tried not to speak to anybody unless I had to; I let sensitivity get the better of me and let my differences control me. I, too, exuded distance. I stood out as a young man knowing he had a strong but irrevocably complex personality, afraid to let that personality breathe for fear of how that personality may manifest in a new environ. And as you may well imagine, I became a very unhappy young man."

Still, Chaucer hadn't answered the question.

"Is not the answer implicit in what I am saying? Two young people can recognise the signs of unhappiness and gravitate toward each other? Her name was Anna."

Surette wondered what she looked like.

"Long, blonde hair; incredible blue eyes and a small oval face with eyes covered with arced lids that helped clarify pain, and a gentle air of sorrow only a kindred spirit could relate to. She was slim, though she wasn't skinny and she was tall though she wasn't lanky. Anna was the most beautiful creature I had ever laid eyes upon. But she, too, spoke to no one - absolutely no one.

Imagine how a girl like that went down amongst the barely pubescent guys at school. She was the talk of the entire place - what she was like; who she spoke to; who she was friendly with; what she wanted. But like I said, she spoke to no one. Anna had chosen isolation as her best means of defence. I had done the same thing. I spoke to no one; she spoke to no one. I spoke to her then she spoke to me.

One knows immediately - to do with outlook, experiences and one's relationship to the world at large. I was in the school library. I was alone. So was she. Eye contact was much to do with curiosity and hesitancy, and much to do with fear. It was not Anna who came to me; I went to Anna. Both of us knew what that the initial approach, either from her, or me, was a matter of formality. My weak words served to break the ice and distract the mind from what the heart was doing without prompting. I wanted to tell her everything; she the same. But fear got in the way and only by increments did we learn. Very soon we were speaking together in the darkest recesses of the library where mutual solace was assured.

Nerves would sometimes get the better of me. We sat down, looked at each other and save for innocuous mumbles, neither of us said anything. Poor words would give way to a knowing silence. With a kindred spirit, words are not qualified to suffice, for only the raw and fragile exteriors of emotion can suffice. And as I looked at Anna, words were truly inadequate. All we had were feelings - soft eyes; tears in our eyes. Often we embraced, knowing that there was something irreducible between us - a question of our earlier lives which we, together, could resolve; a matter of helping each other while surrounded by peoples who just could not have understood."

Chaucer was being vague. He had hardly mentioned what sort of problems Anna professed to have. Surette sensed a tangent coming.

"I have emphasized how my relationship with jazz saved me by allowing my emotions to unveil themselves within sound. What I have not said, up until now, is that if it wasn't for my relationship with Anna, I would have not got to that stage in the first place. We were both seventeen.

We had no one to turn to save for each other. It became a matter of inevitability that we would fall in love."

How?

"By recognising demons; in the times we had together sneaking out of school we would sit and talk when we were sure we wouldn't be seen. The process was slow. Often we would talk about silly things because we would both grow tired of the weight of suffering. Both Anna and I, as you already know, had created structures of counter-reasoning and denial. The past could be explained through reason but the truth isolated from denial would rarely come out. I think, in our early days together, what was implicit was everything. It was only much later that we began to articulate what we had been through. Early on, we were never explicit - it was always meant but unsaid. Whoever said, anyway, that only through the explicitness of words could feelings be transferred?

I knew something was terribly wrong with Anna; for years I wasn't sure exactly what it was. In the beginning, being young and rather naïve although nonetheless caring, I kept looking at her arms and her legs to check for signs of bruising - signs indicative and marks confirmatory of physical abuse. As I could see none, I believed Anna's trauma to be deeper than the rather basic language of beatings and violence used upon me, and altogether more sinister, which it was.

It happened one day when I was least expecting it. Like I said, all of our problems had been dealt with at a subliminal level. She knew of me but not about me. I knew of her but not about her. It was Anna's suggestion that one of us break the ice. Slowly, we began to unveil each other to each other. And slowly we became closer and closer. Mutual therapy if you like. When you get to grow with another person in the way we had grown, the fusion that takes place culls doubt. Anna started telling me of her darkest secrets and me the same, our thoughts became intertwined. We became best friends in the traditional sense and soul mates in whatever sense you wish to take it. You know I often wonder when I see an old couple in a restaurant and they sit in contented silence, how they don't need to speak any more. They can just, be, which seems to me like an ideal state of affairs. Well Anna and I could just, be, and we really didn't care too much thereafter how it was with others. We had found each other.

We represented to the other the first step in the process of being able to let out all of the angst and the insidiousness of our upbringings had defined. Yet we both needed professional help. Getting professional help - I use the word *professional* loosely, was a decision we made together. Each and every time we went to see our psychiatrist we went together - in each others arms."

How old?

"By that time we were eighteen."

Surette asked about sex - sexual relations. Chaucer scowled. Momentarily, Surette thought Chaucer bared his teeth.

"The question is intrusive and the answer personal. Sex is everywhere in this world. Its pervasive nature cheapens intimacy and I wish not, to discuss intimacy, with you. What Anna and I had belonged to us. Credibility here does not belong, nor sustain itself after an excursion into our bedroom."

Surette apologised. He had fallen into the amenable trap of cheap and tardy analysis - the sort he had become used to in passing off banality to the commonplace throng with cheap morals usually plaguing his space; his mind; his couch. The question was offensive and vulgar.

Surette detected a general air of resignation about the Englishman notwithstanding the tender eye smile Surette saw glimpses of. Surette wondered what had happened to Anna. As he was about to ask, Chaucer cut him off. The Englishman looked at his watch.

"Look Doctor; I have to go to Whites."

Chaucer wasn't going to answer the question. Anna Chaucer, evidently, would have to wait.

"When we get back we can talk about Darius Trémé."

Chaucer seemed to be pleading.

"It is so important that we talk about Darius Trémé. There is a great deal to talk about."

Roux Surette was left thinking, musing over the day. Had he learned anything; and what he had learned? He considered Darius Trémé again; thinking about the little boy's family. It was a matter of perspective. Was he concentrating too much on Chaucer and neglecting Darius Trémé? What of Chaucer; what of Darius Trémé?

His wife had often said he was addicted to psychiatry, calling it an unhealthy addiction. Increasingly Surette could feel himself becoming ensconced in the vagaries of Chaucer's story. Perhaps that was to the detriment of Darius Trémé. What was he doing? Time was passing by; time was of the essence. Was Will Chaucer of the essence?

The question was confusing. Everything about the man was confusing. He wrote Chaucer's name on a piece of paper. Next to it he wrote Darius Trémé. Balance, Surette thought - use one and learn from the other. Above all else, remain balanced.

XIII.

How many times must a Doctor relate the slow ebb of life to a relative knowing that all he can offer are weasel words and shallow empathy? How many times had Olivier Godin done exactly the same thing with a distraught mother as another young man had died of a bullet or a blade? The proximity and obviousness of death had hardened Godin's heart; and the Doctor's consoling words got mealier with every lengthening second.

The last days of his father's life were at hand. But Godin could not sit and stew. He had to do something other than wallow by a bed. For the sake of his sanity, inaction was anathema and a Doctor was ignored. He would not stay at his father's side. His father would expect nothing less from a dedicated officer. Godin knew it; his father knew it.

Godin had little idea why Eveny Brien had decided to comfort him. But her presence was in some small way assuring to him, though he wasn't sure why - still her energy; her drive to get him out of there was precisely what he needed.

Soon Godin was back in The Quarter turning his mind to the task in hand. He knew how the Trémé family were feeling. The thought of them softened his heart; so he found the courage to put his feelings to one side and serve the needs of the sufferer. He owed it to the Trémés. He owed it to his father.

Brien dropped Godin off on Royal, close to his destination. And Godin took his place, sitting across the street from Surette's clinic, waiting. Surette was in there with the Englishman, as he could see light emanating from Surette's study window.

Godin found it difficult to concentrate. He constantly looked at the others in the shop, assessing them - at all of The French Quarter types - the tattooed Goth; the plaintive homosexual; the philanthropic family of four; a studious coven of fresh, untainted students. He felt bland and anodyne. How nondescript he was; how his outer shell played a duet with his persona. He wished, just once, that he could assert what he was. He wished he could denude down fear and just, be.

Maybe thirty minutes he waited; maybe an hour. At times, he wanted to leave and return to his father. But his father had all he needed. Godin tried not to wallow. His make-up tried desperately to make him wallow. Forty minutes went by. He decided to leave. His cell phone began to ring. At last, Roux Surette had decided to speak to him, and Surette was rude to the point of persecution.

Surette believed that the killer knew Darius Trémé; the killer was more than likely to strike again; the killer was a male and well known in the higher social circles of New Orleans; the killer knew the Trémés; the boy was murdered because the killer was jealous and harboured a grudge against those likely to enjoy a life of happiness and contentment in a way the killer could not; the killer had a distinct manner and conversational style, making any conversation a stunted conversation, with eye contact held far too long; the perpetrator looking through the object; the object feeling naked, inwardly vilified and outwardly exposed; the killer lived in The French Quarter; the killer mixed successfully and was to a large degree rather popular notwithstanding his social inadequacies; the killer might have a job or a business, which may have engendered respect in the community.

Godin wrote most of it down. Did Surette have an idea who the killer could be? Surette was an intricate part of The French Quarter's nucleus, with an intimate knowledge of most of The French Quarter's characters. Didn't Surette have his own suspicions? How could Surette know so much about the murderer with only a simplistic rhyme to go on, and time spent in the company of an Englishman booked to leave the country in two days time?

The Englishman - how else could these conclusions have been drawn? Surette had no other time on his hands to come up with such an analysis; Surette had been with Chaucer all day.

Godin could only wonder what Scotland Yard would throw his way - enough to substantiate an arrest; to necessitate a charge? As anonymous as New Orleans allowed some to be, there being many hiding in the subterranean nooks and crannies of the city, recognition always followed in the end - a footprint, Godin mused - chaos theory and the footprint - man's infinite variety of traits and the ensuing markers. No one was anonymous. Chaos theory and man, hand in hand; Chaucer had a footprint, and chaos theory would provide.

What if Chaucer was the killer? He had some guts to go into Surette's office and fill the man with a head full of nonsense. Chaucer was the only suspect - circumstantial evidence was better than no evidence at all. But what if circumstantial evidence was, in fact, no evidence at all?

Confusion nagged Olivier Godin. Most killers knew their victims. Chaucer was an outsider. Surette's words dismissed Chaucer as a suspect. It did not make sense. Nothing made sense. Chaucer had somehow duped Surette into believing his own analysis of the pathology of the male, who had killed Darius Trémé, or Chaucer had confessed and Surette was keeping him there for clinical purposes, giving up Will Chaucer when it suited him.

But where was Will Chaucer?

Will Chaucer walked out of Surette's office and head into The Quarter. Godin lost sight of him - a second; a second. His suspect had disappeared.

Godin cut Surette off mid-conversation. He had to. He ran outside and put out a call to the uniforms in The Quarter, detailing a precise description of Will Chaucer, with clear instructions not to approach him. He briefed them all to watch. Godin didn't want him arrested. It was better to wait and observe, remaining vigilant. Godin waited; waiting for confirmation that Chaucer had been spotted. Fifteen minutes - nothing. Another fifteen minutes - nothing.

Surette left the building too. Godin followed him. A hunch? He didn't know. He questioned his motives. Why follow Surette? Why waste time? Was he wasting time? The psychiatrist must recognise the danger he is in. If the killer is certain that Surette can pigeonhole him, then the killer would have every motive in taking the psychiatrist's life. Who was this psychiatrist? Did Surette's credibility in identifying problems, obliterate problems? Did Surette's understanding save Darius Trémé? No. Could

Surette save others? No. Could these inner understandings of the infinitesimal derivations of personality save one person's life? No. Could a deep understanding of the human being even superficially crater the landscape of wickedness? No.

The Englishman was feeding him lines. Why was Surette interested in being fed? What had passed between them that gave Surette the confidence to assert the identity of the killer? What had Surette and Chaucer just discussed?

Godin watched artificial light cascade through Surette's front door and glimpsed the silhouette of Surette's wife. Surette was home; Surette was safe. Godin's mind once again turned to the whereabouts of Will Chaucer. What if he could be eliminated from enquiries? What if he had been found, acting innocently; and acting normally? Godin checked on all his officers on the ground. Chaucer was still missing. The presumption of innocence was beginning to wear thin. He felt it; he knew it - another life was at risk; but where; but when; and by who?

XIV.

Chaucer had looked agitated and seemed restless. When Surette enquired, Chaucer shrugged it off, saying he felt a little oppressed by the humidity on a very humid day, even by the standards of the South.

"Put this inquisition to one side. We need to work together to try to solve this conundrum - the rhyme crafted from the boy's blood."

Surette retrieved the transcript of the note and laid it out on the desk in front of him. Chaucer stood behind and looked over his shoulder. Before they began, Surette buzzed Quinn and asked if the police department had been in touch.

"Not entirely unexpected. Presumably enquiries from the poor discard whose thankless job it is to catch this killer. Have you met him? He isn't here now. You told him to go away; what I would have expected, Doctor. What kind of input do you think a cop could have in a case of this nature? I assume you kept your distance."

Surette and Chaucer read the blood rhyme together. Five minutes passed before either man spoke.

"Doesn't really make that much sense; do you agree? I suppose it was never supposed to make much sense, considering the pathology of the person who wrote it. This is all we have to go on - this pernicious rhyme, is all we have. What do you make of it?"

Surette felt out of his depth. Pride precluded him from wanting to say something stupid but his ego told him to compete. He couldn't hide anymore. Roux Surette wanted to unveil, for if he didn't unveil, Chaucer would smell his own continuous use for Surette's private, selfish, purposes. And Chaucer would come to see him not as some sort of equal partner, but as a useless pug.

So Roux Surette decided to come out; to unveil; to drop his guard; to exhibit the potentiality of weakness and assume a role he was not accustomed to; to subtract the ego attached to his status and retort to Will Chaucer not as a man to be respected and admired for all he had achieved, but, simply, as an educated man who needed help, and an educated man who was willing to accept that help on equal terms.

"My honest opinion?"

Chaucer raised his eyebrow. Surette didn't care.

"Apart from literal meaning, it says very little to me. There are a myriad of ways one could interpret this churlish riddle. If we have to try, then one's starting point is critical. It seems to me that if one starts from the wrong place, then our conclusions will reflect our initial imprecision."

"Correct. But still you have said very little as to what it means. Maybe there are two ways of looking at this dirge. The first is literal; the second is creative. Thus the line....

'a mutant psyche, eviscerating fortune' ....

could be taken literally or we could extrapolate. The meaning of this line is self-evident. If we look for simplicity in each of the lines then the answer may present itself as simplicity."

"This being obvious and simple, then why are we discussing it?"

"The point of being literal is that it forms part of the analytical apparatus we need to use."

"And the rest?"

"Context; what we are left with, notwithstanding the rhyme, is the killer's method in light of this uncouth conundrum; and his method, regardless of this uncouth conundrum."

"So you believe there is some sort of underlying rationale to the torture?"

"Certainly."

Surette couldn't hide his incredulity.

"Doctor; have you ever, in all your years, looked at criminology and penology?

"You mean the study of crime, criminals and the environment?"

"I assume you know what criminology is, but not in any great detail. My detail is lacking, too. I wrote one paper on the subject at Oxford, just to get me through, but, when my stepmother was beating me; and when she was trying to use all sorts of sick psychological terror tactics on me, one thing I did was to read widely.

Are you familiar with medieval methods of punishment and how they have mutated throughout the ages? If you are, you will be only too aware that we have a starting point with which to establish a personality type."

"I know little about medieval punishment. There is little call for that kind of peripheral acumen. Sanctions of that type do not exist in civilised society anymore."

"But we are not talking about civilised society. Civilisation, as such, has no place here. We are being taken back to Europe a few hundred years ago to a time when civilisation bore a close relationship to the simplicity of inter-personal brutality and brutality against the person handed down by the state, or, nominally, the King."

Chaucer sounded conclusive - conclusiveness which infused Surette with insecurities as to whether Chaucer was actually talking down to him. Paradoxically, Surette still wanted to know more - to understand; to learn. He wanted information - a thirst for information marking his natural inquisitiveness, even if inquisition had been eroded somewhat by his own arrogance.

"The atrocities visited upon Darius Trémé are similarly visited upon hundreds of thousands of people each and every year. Victims live in a uncivilised world given that the majority still see the infliction of pain to the body as just recompense."

"Are you assuming the perpetrator of this crime is a man who emanates from a more civilised environ? Or are you assuming the opposite?"

"Why should we assume anything? I'll tell you why the killer is from a civilised world. It is the systematic way the torture was conducted and the knowledge-aforethought we can derive from the act. Darius Trémé had his stomach ripped open with a scalpel. His intestines were unravelled before his eyes while he was hanging from a mahogany beam. His intestines were cut and burned. That is a starting point. The evisceration resembles the medieval ritualistic punishment of quartering prevalent in England in the fifteenth century.

Darius Trémé had his skin lacerated at points designed to inflict maximal pain with the killer using pincers to create knots and holes in the fabric of his skin; holes which were then filled with boiling sulphur and such like. That particular method of punishment was prevalent in France at the same time quartering was adopted in England.

Then there are the ropes - ropes that dislocated Darius Trémé's limbs, ensuring that the boy died in the most excruciating pain. There are any number of countries where ritualistic dislocation has been practised. It originates in Europe in the Middle Ages because it exists alongside the psychology of punishment that existed in Europe in the Middle Ages. This is the punishment of the body for the sins of the mind, Doctor - the punishment of the body, for the sins of the mind."

"But why a child?"

"That, unfortunately, is more difficult. Once we have established a method to the evisceration of that boy, then we have a start."

"What about Darius Trémé's heart? Why was his heart removed? What was the reason Darius Trémé's heart was skewered with the message we are looking at now? Why was the boy hung? Why were his hands burnt off with sulphur? It does not seem to me we are asking and answering any of the right questions here. You may have answers for a selection of the litany of punishments the boy suffered but not all of them. Why have you chosen some mutilations but not all?"

Chaucer smiled.

"Well I have and I haven't. The simple answer is that I don't have all of the answers. I do recognise enough behind the suffering meted out to the Trémé boy that, on the balance of probabilities, my reasoning as to the nature of evisceration and murder, should start with the psychology of punishment itself. So let us assume for one moment that I am correct.

We have established that the killer had a purpose. We now know that the killer's activities reflect a barbarity akin to Medieval Europe hundreds of years ago, in particular England and France, although this in no way precludes the other countries of Europe at the time. We can at least assume that the killer did not invent these punishments out of thin air but has read widely.

If boy's killer has read quite widely then the man is not under-educated. No; this person fits right into his particular social strata. In fact, it will prove difficult to establish any obvious difference from the killer and the society the man inhabits. Possibly, the knowledge of punishment and its rationale is information the killer comes into contact with as part of a job."

"Like a history teacher for example?"

"Precisely."

"What about the words of the rhyme, which doesn't seem to be a conundrum really. It only seems to be a cryptic reflection of the killer's past and what the killer has done. Am I right?"

Chaucer was pensive. Surette could sense him trying to make his mind up.

"The methods of evisceration used suggest a medieval ritual akin to the Elizabethan period. If this is so, the killer must have a mind so organised in its own axiomatic madness to be able to compartmentalise punishment and to give punishment meaning, no matter how vile you and I think the punishment is. Consider the criminal offence of murder. Consider a system where the criminal's body was advertently punished for the sins of the body and the mind - both, being a criminality consequence of the proclivities of the mind. Consider how the body was punished in extreme cases with the public and ritualistic execution of the murderer - how he was hung, drawn, quartered, flayed, skinned, eviscerated and killed.

Vanity; the point is to do with vanity. The killer is confronting whatever he carries inside and saying that this is who I am, what I have always been and this is what I have done and intend to continue doing. A switch has been flicked. The killer's self-repression has been overcome. A madman wants to tell the world. But there is telling the world with torture and the taking of life, and there is telling the world through the cryptic nature of that note.

Now that we have a sense of background, we can look at the note in such a way as to clarify at least some of the killer's intentions, notwithstanding the vanity I have already mentioned."

Chaucer smiled. The smile was rather more genuine than the loaded facial expressions Surette had grown used to. For all Chaucer's protestations of a sinister pathology, there seemed to be gentleness about him, a moral purpose and a kindness which went against what Surette believed was his intrinsic nature. It posed a question as to the nature of the origin of morality itself, for here was a man with no reason to be anything other than a violent pig, behaving in the contrary manner. Why?

"Your remit is only to provide a psychological profile of the killer, not to catch the killer. Once we are done here, you will no doubt hand over your report to the New Orleans Police Department."

"Difficult; this is a police force with an unenviable record of corruption and incompetence."

"So what do you propose? The New Orleans Police Department seems to be the only conduit available. I would remind you that you only have to profile the killer's pathology. Once you have done that, then your job over, is it not?"

Surette disagreed.

"You want to enhance your own prospects and profile by being seen to snare the killer yourself? But whoever did this to Darius Trémé is extremely dangerous. Is that a risk you are willing to take? Or, are you saying you want him for clinical purposes only?"

Chaucer had struck a nerve. And he knew it.

"So you do. Surely the killer must be brought to justice? If you attempt to do this in isolation you will not get very far. The killer can blend into the community and has probably blended into the community for some considerable time - difficult to spot; difficult to know. You are attempting to transcend the law. You really do need the police on your side.

Anyhow; this basic rhyme. I would say it also reflects, in part, jealousy. At face value it reveals the eyes of a man who detests an environment he has not been allowed access to. Try not to imagine you are one of the bankers, lawyers, Prozac addicts, gin victims and God knows what else, who come in here to expose their unkempt souls. Think of yourself as one of those dirty and unkempt black jazz musicians with their battered brass instruments congregating in Jackson Square in The Quarter. Imagine how you would think, as you saw the Caucasians in suits with Cuban cigars stuck to their bottom lip, indulging you with fifty cents or a dollar for some stunning performance of an old jazz standard. How would you feel if all you ever wanted to be was just like the people who indulged you with their change?

You could be bitter and twisted; you could be angry. You could commit crime against the person and the property of those with more than you, be they black or white. Or, you could choose not to buck the system. You make the choice to allow the system work for you from a more formal perspective - you go to school; you try to work hard at school;

Yet, ultimately you fail and whether you tried to better yourself or not, you still end up playing a battered trombone all day in Jackson Square because you have no choice. Poverty and Jackson Square are your destiny. You will always be poor. Destitution, resignation and hopelessness become a way of life.

Let us say that you have the ability to recognise that you never stood a chance of getting out; of getting away from the environment in which you are trapped. Provided the seeds of hatred are there in the beginning, they will fester and rot; they will gestate and they will mutate you until one day they come out in a way which satiates the hatred because it passes the buck. Hatred is transposed to the victim and to the innocent. So look at the rhyme again. See what I see? What do you, think?"

"I am a black man and a black man who is on any criteria, a success. That the black man wasn't destined to making ends meet is utterly incorrect. America has travelled a long way in the recent past. Sure; subjugation still exists, and subliminal racism is everywhere, but to strike down all with the stroke of a pen, is just plainly incorrect. The South has a lot to answer for; and the South is my home. I make no apologies for who I am. Why should I? And life on Jackson Square is not an absolute - not these days."

"I get your point. In making your point, all you have done is allow me to establish that you have not got mine. We are not in some general social commentary on the social mobility of peoples being dependent upon the colour of their skin. What we are dealing with in the context of this rhyme is the psychology of one human being trying to explain how he looks at the world and how the world has stopped him seeking release from the urges which have culminated in the death of Darius Trémé.

Can you see how the parallels are the same - release; release and jealously - the need for legitimate achievement denied the black man and the need for legitimate release denied to the killer. The result is an equivalent - rejection or acceptance. Or compromise until matters get too much."

Surette could see how compromise was of paramount importance - compromise denuding excess. If Chaucer's analysis was correct, the killer was free of his former constraints; the killer now had a taste for it; and the killer would not stop at one.

"You are wondering whether any man who shows these vestiges of madness has the capacity to examine and know whether he is morally right or morally wrong. You are assuming such an examination requires reason, and the man who murdered that boy because that man murdered that boy, has no rational side to him.

Look; I am not unique. My actions are, or have been wrong and I have chosen, in order to get on, to curtail my urges. The killer has to some extent managed to curtail his urges otherwise many other deaths of this nature would have arisen over time.

Take this line again....

.... a mutant psyche, eviscerating fortune....

So whose fortune is the killer eviscerating? Who has the mutant psyche? What kind of fortune is the killer eviscerating?

Let's assume that the killer is eviscerating the good fortune of Darius Trémé and our killer is the bearer of a mutant psyche. Hence, the killer is entirely self-aware of his murderous nature and his potential.

And what kind of fortune are we realising here? Is Darius Trémé the victim as he has potential or actual fortune?"

"I fail to see any difference."

"The difference is critical. We have to make judgements as to what the killer sees. We have already established that this murder was committed by an individual who is incarcerated by urges and capable of analysing those urges. This is an allocation of a fair degree of reflective intelligence - reflective intelligence looking upon the fortune of a child and obliterating that child.

To harm the boy based on actual fortune suggests opportunism. Most murders are opportunistic. What may have happened is that the killer's urges just enveloped him at a particular moment in time - Darius Trémé being in the wrong place; Darius Trémé an affluent white boy from a well-to-do New Orleans family and just the kind of boy a twisted mind would want to damage as compensation for the hideousness of the existence itself. But this wouldn't make sense because this murder was way too pre-meditated.

The boy was killed because of potential fortune, not actual fortune. Darius Trémé clearly exhibited all of the traits which suggested to the killer that Darius Trémé was going to enjoy precisely the kind of future life that the killer has never had.

Whoever did this watched Darius Trémé and made a judgement. He then chose to harm the boy because jealousy of the boy's potential happiness was just too much for the killer to handle. This was not an opportunistic crime; and this was no sick sort of sex crime either. The evisceration and murder of the boy was, in part, simple and basic jealousy."

"The killer knew Darius Trémé?"

"Darius Trémé was seen letting himself into his parent's home; there was no evidence that entry to the Trémé's residence was forced; there was no evidence of struggle within the house although granted, Darius Trémé was only seven years of age and the killer must have been bigger and stronger; no money was taken; neither jewellery nor any other expensive items were removed from the property; the child was not sexually abused in any way; the killer was methodical; the killer planned this programmatic death because the method is tested. This took time to plan and undertake. Time was going to be a crucial factor but if the killer knew Darius Trémé, and that he normally spent a couple of hours on his own, after school, then the killer has the intelligence to execute his plan.

Doctor; you must tell this Detective, Olivier Godin; you must tell him you believe the man who killed Darius Trémé was well acquainted with the boy. Indeed, you must tell him the killer was well acquainted with the boy's parents too. And you must forget your rather selfish assumptions that you will be able to snare this killer. You are not qualified to hunt and catch this man. The New Orleans Police Department are. You will be obviating your responsibilities if you do not tell this Detective, Olivier Godin, that the killer knew Darius Trémé. More importantly you will be putting other children in The French Quarter at risk should you not let Olivier Godin get on with his job. Knowing that the killer knew Darius Trémé narrows the search down to a tiny fraction of what it could have been. It also means that you are likely to know the individual who killed the boy."

"Impossible. Surely I would have suspected."

"The social circle you are likely to mix in within the professional élite is quite small. Though The French Quarter is but a small part of the New Orleans infrastructure, it represents the essence of New Orleans in all things. I believe the killer must be around or within the sort of social circles frequented by the Trémé family and yourself too. It wouldn't surprise me that you or your wife or some of your close friends will be acquainted with the man."

Surette was angry at the implicit assumption that he did not have the ability to recognise the evil potential of the man who killed the Trémé's boy. Was Will Chaucer the only man baptized with the right to know who was and who wasn't genuine or honest?

Besides, the upper echelons of the New Orleans professional community was not the sort of place were a man could survive for years, hiding a secret from others. There were no secrets in The French Quarter. The élite would get to know him intimately. Everybody's business was your business simply because The French Quarter was so socially claustrophobic. Separation and secrecy was, outside the confines of marriage, practically impossible.

Surette knew many, if not all the secrets of the New Orleans élite. He found it impossible to believe the killer had at some point in time, sat upon his couch and failed to unveil a sinister, murderous pathology.

"Of course he wouldn't have made an appearance here. Think; the rhyme is a gateway to the way the killer thinks of himself. The killer has a deal of reflective intelligence. It may be that the killer has tried to get some sort of help or assistance in the past, but if you carry a murderous proclivity in your breast for the majority of your thinking life, the very last person you would be unveiling it to would be somebody who knows you. My guess is that you would not, in fact, be unveiling it at all."

"Why then; why now?"

"There lies another clue to the identity of the killer. Perhaps that should be a matter for you to pass on. Try to look for someone known to the Trémé family who has suffered some recent, overt trauma, bereavement or some other significant loss. Look for anything that may have formed the catalyst changing the killer's internal dialogue from simply one of thought, to one of thought and resulting action.

If we can establish that someone out there has been through an appropriate form of overt trauma, then we might be a bit closer to grabbing a suspect or indeed several suspects."

Surette didn't like the sound of that. There would be no grabbing of one or indeed several suspects until he was sure they had the right man. He could not, on the basis of Will Chaucer's partly specious partly rational argument, have Godin grabbing well-to-do people off the street.

"Why not? Afraid are we; afraid that the well-heeled will start pointing the finger at you if you start advising Godin to arrest and interrogate totally innocent people? You think there is politics in this? Need I not remind you that while you consider sweeping up after yourself, another child will die. And you want to get political over things?

If it helps isolate and catch this killer, my opinion is that every civil person in The French Quarter should be willing to submit themselves to a lie detector and DNA test and do their civil duty. What have any of them got to lose, save for one of their children?"

Surette changed the subject, returning to the rhyme.

"Perhaps you should tell me, Doctor, as all of this is going to be on your head when you can't turn around and classify the killer. Or, you let me continue because all I want to do is stop another child being murdered whereas all you want is to stop the death-knell of your career by not pissing off the natives. So we should return to the note attached to the body."

Chaucer had pegged Surette for what he was - self-interested; not the valuable reference point for so many of the high powered individuals in New Orleans but a self-important parasite who preyed upon the weaknesses of middle class and moneyed America.

Chaucer had shown him the fundamental weakness in his outlook - a selfish, narcissism resulting in analytical dearth and settling for a dishonest appraisal of the world around him. Surette had made the easy choices - seeing his name above his office door; the letters after his name; his name in the newspapers; his name on the tips of the tongues of The French Quarter; but without empathy for a dead boy; unable to put the need for retribution and deterrence before his desire to learn of the human mind - self before all and the remnants of a dead child. Chaucer was a complex man, and in many ways, a very unfortunate man. Through stress and duress, a man had emerged - a better man than he. Yes; putting aside his arrogance; putting aside the ego developed under his self-identity as a man of self-proclaimed importance; putting aside his fear and concern over and above concerns for catching the killer, Roux Surette had to admit, if nothing else, he had developed a significant degree of respect for Will Chaucer.

Reliance, he well knew, came through trust; and somehow, Surette was beginning to trust the Englishman. Now he questioned himself - why; why because it seemed as if all Will Chaucer had ever done was question and analyse to the boundaries of all against all and by fighting against the iniquity of all he had endured, Chaucer was a man in control; a man in charge, when, at first, that destiny had been given with the urges and desire to use violence fed to him by his stepmother before he was old enough to know better; a man of honesty and of integrity.

"I have to be back at Whites again. I can get you the best table in the restaurant. We have talked jazz an awful lot, especially this morning. Why don't you come to the restaurant for our performance tonight? Let me see if I am able to convince you that there is more rather than less to jazz than meets the ear. Why don't you bring your wife? That's it; it is settled then. I insist."

Surette wanted to decline. He should have said no. For some reason, he didn't.

'From mind, to eye, to body,

Spittle violence is served around;

A mutant psyche, eviscerating fortune,

Damning all profound'"....

Chaucer spat out the words. His voice was all-consuming, powerful and cock-sure.

"Something interests me specifically. It is to do with this first line,

.... 'From mind, to eye, to body'....

Imagine the penetrative urge of the killer. Imagine a killer knowing that inside him dwells an insidious virus that permeates all he knows. He has to establish he is the only one or not the only one. Why? In order to define himself, he has be different and will stare; will look right through you, assessing your differences; the eyes - how they confirm or not, that you harbour secret perceptions; harmful perceptions; searching for matters tangible - weaknesses and strengths; like young men who look to the body and estimate physical prowess.

We are not, I believe, dealing with a young man. We are dealing with a highly sophisticated older man. The line 'from mind to eye to body' is his way of trying to tell us how he has resolved his differences in the past; how he has chosen to deal with the social world he inhabits now."

Surette had had enough.

"The bottom line is that we are looking for a man who is intense - incredibly intense; perhaps not in terms of appearance, but someone who will give clues to their thought processes and their mannerisms?"

"Overlong eye contact; glazed watery eyes - glazed at the point of entry into a conversation; an over association with detail; pickiness; as if the individual were trying to work out in exact terms what was going on inside the head of the other, clarifying on a back-stock of core knowledge of all others then asking if the person they are talking to fits into a recognisable pattern.

It is the little things - we have a man trying to work out precisely who he is and what he is. And it is addictive. These are thought processes that can never stop; will never leave this killer. We have a mind configured to find out how and why it is so."

Like Chaucer himself.

"Yes Doctor; in a way - this man is a bit like me but without the same control as I have - without the same level of control."

"And the rest of this rhyme - it fits a pattern?"

.... 'Spittle violence served around'....

Can you see how that works?"

"The action of spitting is a challenge; a challenge to those who would dare to step in the way? Basically you are right."

"So it is a challenge?"

"Yes; it is a challenge. The question is whether the rhyme is a challenge to anyone in particular or to whomever may have the unenviable task of standing in this man's way. My guess is that the killer had no one in mind. The killer left the rhyme as a medium of knowing for the right analytical person, without knowing who that would be.

The killer is also playing games. It is a line in the sand saying, here I am and yes, I have committed the most hideous crime against an innocent boy. I will continue to do so until one of you fools gets the message. I am amongst you; I will remain amongst you until I am caught.

"Presumably the killer will become more and more frustrated as time goes by, should he not be caught?"

"Now that his persona has altered, all the perpetrator of this crime wants to do is to come out to one and all and state - this is what I am, this is what I have been my whole life and this, finally, is what you, have to deal with."

XV.

From the browning classroom window, all Mia Laval could see was people; was adults; was important and sad people; were parents waiting for their children to leave school; parents waiting to take them all to safety; to the safety of home.

Mia could see television cameras; could see reporters with notebooks and expensive phones calling others and telling a story to the world. And like all the children looking through classroom glass, Mia Laval did not know why school, or the children, should be the centre of everybody else's world; of her, world.

Bits of her found it exciting - just bits though - exciting - it was exciting to see so many people with so many cameras and so much to say. But Mia Laval knew that something was wrong; that something was not right. She knew something awful had happened, even though she did not know for sure what could be so, so, awful.

She had been sad all day - sensing pain - loss - combinations of actions leading to pain and loss, pain and longing; just rumours circulating school all day - the way they looked and how they spoke; behaviour and people adding up to more than how they appeared when they were alone - each part adding to the mix and the mix feeding Mia's senses. Something was wrong. Something terrible had taken place. She knew. She knew.

She hated the attention. She wanted to go home and avoid the attention. It wasn't exciting really. Mia was scared. She wanted to forget what she had heard. She wanted her mother and father. She wanted out; she wanted to be alone; of doing things for her; of being happy; of being young; of being an innocent child.

The refreshing innocence of childhood and the inner-decency of an upbringing fraught with love; with affection - Mia would ascend to adulthood; a flourishing career; a stable life - how her parents taught her to embellish their love with a mind of her own; the feelings gifted to her in the fresh air of youth prefacing a friendly and welcoming world.

Mia was the brightest pupil in her class. A considerate and caring child; a child simply following her parent's lead – that everybody is equal before God; that intellect is nothing without compassion; that faith is triumph and God the master of all - all embedded within Mia and colouring her inquisitive mind, without controlling her inquisitive mind. For what God had chosen to give Mia had been afforded others in equal portions in different ways; and no one on Earth had the right to look down; and no one had the obligation to look up.

Why, then, would a child like Mia Laval question the world in which she lived? Why would she question her parent's good intentions? They were wonderful people - a surgeon; a nurse; both part-time lay preachers in the Anglican Church. God was on their side; God would look after them.

Mia buttoned up her coat and collected her assignments. Mia Laval was the happiest girl in the world - the ideal child; the unmitigated, undiluted, uninhibited, categorical, ideal child.

What a sad day a happy child had born witness to. It had started many hours earlier. It had started before school had started. Her mother took a call and shed tears at the breakfast table. Faces were sad. Her father was a ghost - white; quiet - not his usual self at all. Her mother held her close all the way to school, making sure she was alright, and happy, even though Mia didn't feel happy, because her mother wasn't happy.

It wasn't just her mother's behaviour, either. Other mothers, who wouldn't normally walk their children to school, were pressing face cheeks against sons and daughters in the French Quarter morn.

Mia and her friends looked on, bemused; somewhat distraught mothers and distracted fathers carried handkerchiefs snivelling and wiping their shiny, red noses as they wept and tried to hide their sadness from the children.

There were the words of her cruel and dishonest classmates. Something terrible had happened to Darius Trémé. Darius Trémé would not be coming to school. He had left school. He would not be coming back. Darius Trémé had been expelled. Darius Trémé would not be going to school because his father was going to prison for stealing money and Darius Trémé had to go live in a home where bad children go.

Mia's mom hugged Mia for the last time. She squeezed Mia's best friend too. When Mia asked why she was crying, tears rolled down her mother's smooth cheeks, soaking the shallow collars of her black silk shirt.

The images frustrated Mia; it maddened her; made her mad; made her angry. She wanted to help. Mia Laval's mother wouldn't talk about it;

Mia Laval's mother said she couldn't talk about it. And that frustrated Mia Laval terribly too. And school was miserable.

An assembly was called first thing. Principal Brossard tried to explain how Darius Trémé would not be attending school anymore. There had been an awful tragedy. Some of the teachers had big, red eyes.

Principal Brossard talked about bravery and loss. How odd it should be that her headmaster was talking about loss in relation to Darius Trémé, when he had not said that anything had happened to Darius Trémé, save for that there had been a tragedy.

Some of the boys, who were known to be rather cruel, were telling hideous stories about Darius Trémé and what had been done to him. Mia was afraid. What if the stories about Darius Trémé were true?

She waited in line to leave. Elaborate arrangements had been made to make sure that all the children were safe. Mia's mother, who had to be at work, made a specific request of the teacher, Mrs. Surette that Mia was to be taken home by the parents of one of Mia's best friends; that Mia should be taken to her own front door and locked in the house until her mother returned.

Something terrible must have happened to Darius Trémé. Mia asked Mrs. Surette, who normally answered all of her questions. Now, apparently, wasn't the right time to be asking questions. Mia stopped asking.

Then she was being pushed past the people outside. Mia was surprised at just how many police officers she saw. And they were not just outside her school gates. Mia had never seen so many police officers in The French Quarter - fat and mean men; rude men pushing them, examining them, controlling them.

Mom's friend opened the front door of their house on Chartres Street. Mia was soon locked in; and happy to be sitting in front of the open log fire that burnt in Winter, still smelling of burnt wood in Summer, reminding her of the snow that fell last fall.

Warmth and comfort - something to her localé Mia had always felt happy with. Familiarity; something in the way the house was; the fall of the curtains, the hearth, colours and smells. Mia was content; Mia was happy.

Maybe contentment dulls the mind and denudes the senses; maybe so, for when Mia heard the doorbell she completely forgot the strict instructions Mrs. Surette had given her - that she was to open the front door to no one; that she was not to show her face to any of the windows of the house should anyone knock at the front door; that if anyone knocked at the front door she was to call 911 immediately.

Maybe contentment led her to believe that there could be nothing sinister out there; and nothing sinister in the face and of the personality of the person she opened the door to.

Mia Laval would always open the door to a friendly face; she would open the door to someone she had known for most of her life; a face; the only face Mia Laval would know for the rest of her life.

That face for its smile; that face to do with goodness, and kindness. Why should she expect anything different from that face now? No such memory; no such mind. Mia Laval couldn't remember that which isn't so. And what she could have remembered was soon lost; memories discarded through surprise; through the immediacy of astonishment; through pain; through what was there and then.

There; and then, she saw her arm being squeezed and twisted above the elbow. She was dragged into the living room. She saw her face in the hall mirror as she was dragged past, seeing incredulity, unknowing, puzzlement as to why the actions and the demeanour of the person she had let into the house, of the person she had totally trusted, had turned into those of a monster.

She saw the glint of the blade plunged into the hearth fire, now alight. She caught the smell of sulphur cascaded through the room when it started to boil. She saw ropes strung up over the beams which dissected the room.

Unknowing had cleared to a path to unveil the horror of what Darius Trémé had suffered. And Mia Laval realised for the first time how the pain she was feeling in her arms was not a dream; not a nightmare; it was real; she, was real; the knife was real; the pain, was real.

So Mia Laval did the only thing her weak and small frame could do in the face of this strong and aggressive adult - Mia struggled; Mia begged; Mia pleaded. How she struggled; how she begged until she could plead no more. How she screamed - glass-cracking pain-filled screams at the top of her voice; interminable screams stripping the skin off her tonsils; screams which ran to the hysterical when her screams were laughed back at her and she was slapped with such force that she flew across the room, falling unconscious.

And how things were different when she was woken up with a fist, this time to the temple; being told how inconsiderate it was to fall unconscious when all around her things were beginning to take shape.

Mia could now see ropes which hung from the central beam above her. She looked at a pot of boiling sulphur and wax which hung over the fire below the hearth. She felt numb. She didn't understand; couldn't grasp the all around. Mia stopped asking 'why' because all was beyond all she knew; beyond everything before. It wasn't just the pain from the beatings which had been administered - pain as Mia had never felt before; it was the anticipation; the need which Mia sensed in the maniacal eyes that looked deep into hers; it was the change in those eyes - eyes which Mia Laval had looked into many times. She was being stripped bare. Her little personality was being looked into, watched and, controlled.

Mia Laval did the only thing left to her. Mia cried. The eyes in front of her bawled too. They cried together.

Mia was dragged by the hair, picked up and placed within the ropes which hung a couple of feet away from the fire. She was tied to those ropes so tightly that the pain to her wrists and ankles caused her to cry out loud, until a knife was inserted into her mouth and her tongue cut out. The ropes attached to her limbs were pulled tighter and tighter and her eyes began to see white flashes of light and the pain in her head became intense.

Mia had stopped understanding. Her head began to hang as her legs and arms were dislocated, and her joints at the point of dislocation had swelled to grotesque enormity. Her remaining clothes were ripped from her body by a surgical scalpel. She was strung up naked, and pincers so hot that they glowed orange were used to pull and fry discordant lumps flesh from her thighs and her arms before boiling wax and sulphur was poured into the holes wherein a child's flesh once was. When a handkerchief was removed from her mouth so as to stop her from swallowing too much of her own blood, she obeyed gravity as her powerless neck allowed her head to fall forward once more.

Her arms and her legs were stretched. Still her torturer looked into her eyes; looked into Mia's eyes as their light began to fade, until the time was right for Mia to look down and see her stomach cut and ripped open by a scalpel penetrating to her intestines which were pulled out and unravelled before her. As Mia saw, Mia felt - astonishment. Astonishment.

Then followed the smell - then the smell as sulphur was poured upon her intestines and they began to burn; a smell like no other that child had taken into her lungs. As Mia Laval felt life seep away, she saw the scalpel being plunged deep into her chest wall. She felt her throat being squeezed by the noose and as the noose tightened the sight of her heart before her eyes, still attached to her body, as the flashes of pain and white light turned into caverns of darkness - her heart cut from her as the rope around her neck tightened and a dull crack told that Mia Laval's neck had broken; and life had left her body. Mia Laval was dead.

And wherever Mia Laval's soul went to next, she would have seen the desecration continue; that the subsequent desecration was different from that of Darius Trémé - how her heart was nailed to the beam and attached to the nail was a rhyme; how her head was severed although the noose was allowed to remain around her neck; how Mia Laval's brain was removed from within her skull and nailed to the wall.

Finally, the killer looked at what was left of the body and conducted a close examination of the scene. Any clues were meant clues. The killer left the building, and certain matters became certain - the shallow smile; the replete smile which briefly crossed the killer's face seemed to cut away flesh, bone; to cut away sinew and expose the icy inner countenance of the perpetrator of this second, hideous crime. A little girl was dead. And a killer's life was the better for it.

XVI.

Emily and Roux Surette ignored the queue, stepped into Whites and were ushered to the best table in the house, next to the stage. Behind them and waiting were the usual mixed throng of music lovers - people Surette mostly thought of as fools - how they soiled the Quarter; better that they sit behind, he thought, it would be easier to concentrate on Chaucer.

Surette was soon spotted - waiting staff mostly; with whispered opinions as to whether Surette should be in a restaurant enjoying himself while Darius Trémé's killer was somewhere in the Quarter. Surette scoffed; these tips and favours waiters would not jeopardise employment and high season income by publicly challenging a man many of them knew in private. And the ambient mumblings soon reverted to the normal clatter and social growl of a busy bar, a hungry restaurant and an anticipatory clientele.

There were reasons he was there; reasons beyond the veil of the Quarter's skewed gossip and rumour dictat. Surette looked around; he looked around just like the previous evening. Last night he saw nothing;

felt nothing; became nothing as he read of the slaying of Darius Trémé. Tonight, in a crowded room, he saw no one; no one save for his beloved wife, Emily.

If Surette had looked closely, he may have seen Olivier Godin propping up the bar, far from the stage, backed off and hugging the darkness in a corner. Calculations; if Surette did see him, so be it, but it wouldn't help Godin's cause if he did. Better to preserve his anonymity; better to live in semi-permanent light; better to watch and to learn. Chaucer was not to see him talking to Surette; Chaucer was there to be seen consorting with Surette, after the set.

Godin's trip to Whites had already been fruitful. Chaucer was back stage. He had been missing for a couple of hours. But there were no reports of anything untoward in The Quarter. If bad news did reach him, Godin was proximate to the only suspect. An arrest of the man, albeit publicly, would follow.

Arrest or not, Godin had the chance to watch Chaucer from close quarters - the option of trying to obtain a more definitive impression; of validating Surette's obsession. Roux Surette's presence was a bonus. If Chaucer and Surette spoke; if Surette and the Englishman interacted, Godin could gauge an impression, an opinion, a chance to confirm or discard.

Surette, on the other hand, was thinking about his family; his children; his parents. The young ones were safe, happy with their grandparents in the family house in The Garden District, just a few miles away. Then there was Emily, his wife, sitting next to him, waiting for the evening to begin. Would she enjoy what was to follow? She had shown little interest in jazz - almost no interest in music of any type. Emily's feeling for sound was peripheral to her life force - no known inclination to hear live music, which was, after all, a New Orlean locus; and she had never used music to effect release of any sort. She never sang. She had never danced.

Another frosty stare from an adjacent table; but Surette understood - concerned punters questioning his presence - fools; simple patient diagnostics - Chaucer in Chaucer's space; Chaucer on home ground and just too good an opportunity to miss; the heart of the man; a substantiation of Chaucer's thesis about jazz; about astonishment and about music's supposedly superior relationship with the inner man. Like fingerprints; like snowflakes, man is an infinite variety of type, motive and imagination structure - get one who is clever and gifted, then knowledge is power and another step is undertaken.

Then again, Roux Surette was only too aware of Darius Trémé - the monkey crawling all over his back. Choose not to attend Whites; lose Chaucer's input; and another life may be lost in The French Quarter. Then comes the blame; then comes his downfall prefaced by the attractant intoxication in not knowing, like a feeble woman besotted with the contradictory wiles of a manipulative suitor - this element of unknowing; this lodestar of addiction - mystery the benefactor of diffidence; and diffidence the adversary of progress.

Surette had been around jazz his whole life, discounting Harvard and that year at Oxford. How he detested the relentless way jazz was used to identify the black man. So what if he was black? So what if jazz and the colour of his skin had some potted sable history? Escape the label; so to escape the connotations of being a black man in New Orleans - a label supposedly dictating his actions. Escape indeed.

The label was insulting. The colour-of-skin connotations were insulting. He had earned his respect on his terms - the right to be respected by all members of the community so forget skin; forget, soul; forget sound.

Sound as Chaucer called it - the key to unlocking the dark recesses of the soul; the oblique fusion of experience in those who had no opportunity to let experiences breathe in other ways - the key to venting anger, assuaging maltreatment, abuse, destruction, mourning, loss, pain, suffering and transgression for those lucky enough to have the musical facility to do it - Chaucer himself, in Chaucer's very words.

Surette may have had little relationship to music because he had no musical talent, but was it because he didn't have the ears' intricate infrastructure Chaucer was gifted with, or did his hatred of jazz arise as he was the happy recipient of a decent upbringing and positive outlook? What was it Chaucer had said - experience; experience - a word with a myriad of meanings; so why, did Chaucer's talent mean more than this to so many?

Surette consoled himself. Chaucer's proclamations were only relevant when trying to establish the thoughts, motives and traits of a psychopath who had killed and mutilated a seven-year-old boy. And such self proclamation was hardly going to get one a job as head of state, head of a corporation, a bar tender or a garbage collector - experience; self delusion; self as the centre of all; experience, and the deluded self - Will Chaucer.

Surette looked at Emily. What would she think of Chaucer? What would she have made of the faces of the crowd during Chaucer's performance last night - how Chaucer had the audience travel; at the way they lost their environment; at the way their eyes glazed as conversation stopped and eye contact between lovers and companions in a private world of colliding thought and feeling.

In as much as he could see, and to a degree, feel how Will Chaucer's playing had the ability to transform the human condition, although it had failed to transform his own, Chaucer had a little of the capacity to relate to and infuse through sound, the self-expression his past had engendered. Surette was thus willing to admit part of his jealousy came from inadequacy in that he could empathise with his patients but he couldn't, through the solutions he offered, get to the very substance of human experience - the human experiences of everyone who sat on his couch. Chaucer had the ability to push his way into the human condition just by blowing selected notes down and out of one end of a brass musical instrument to the other. To Roux Surette, that didn't make sense, because it couldn't make sense. On the contrary, it was nonsense.

Emily seemed to be enjoying herself. Surette admitted that Whites was a wonderfully intimate place, infused as it was with all the darker tones of rouge and burgundy against candlelight and darkened wood, juxtaposed by the sight and the smells of the food and the manner and character of New Orleans indigent people. Surette still loved Louisiana; he loved New Orleans; he loved it; he loved the people - the people he felt part of whether they wanted him tonight or not.

How beautiful she was. How poised and elegant. How innocent was Emily Surette; how beautifully innocent. He remembered their first meeting, all those years ago.

They met by accident. Surette was sitting in a bar in The Quarter; a bar long since gone, on the corner of Chartres and Toulouse. He hadn't long returned from Oxford, and was waiting on his exam results. So were his parents who had come to join him, certain to order the champagne once the news was confirmed, as it was. With Surette holding a glass in his hand, champagne warming his throat, in walked this rather young, tall, elegant but dirty - yes that was the word - dirty, woman, who trundled to the bar carrying two suitcases, undernourished, weak; and in need of help.

Surette's mother saw Emily first. Maise Surette was a nurse and read all of the requisite signs of poor feeding and neglect. She put her arm around Emily, as the weight of the suitcases caused her to stumble. Young and naïve, Roux Surette wasn't sure what to do. His mother ordered him to get Emily some food.

She said she had not eaten for two days and ate like it, somehow avoiding Surette's feeble and awkward questions - a stray and a pedigree, circling. And that was how the relationship had started - over time; a long time - Roux Surette about to start work as a junior doctor on the wards of the New Orleans University Hospital, and Emily charged by Roux Surette's mother to stay at their familial home until a decision that she was well enough to leave.

Surette recalled a strange relationship; a friendship that seemed to grow out of necessity with both of them the same age. He was awkward, bookish and a man who hadn't flowered at all. He was all Emily had, and Emily had grown into him, and flowered quickly in many ways.

They had grown together. Emily turned out to be amusing, cynical and rather dry. But she was very loving and forever grateful for the kindness and affection she was showered with. Emily was a woman without sides, scrupulously honest, attentive and above all else, she loved Surette without qualification.

There seemed to be only one rule with Emily. And she was adamant - it was never to be discussed between them the reasons why she had ended up in New Orleans, destitute and homeless. And so, Roux Surette fell in love with her. And he had never brought the subject up once in all the years they had spent together, which, as Surette reflected in those few quiet moments he had to himself in Whites, had been good years - wonderfully good years.

Falling in love; learning to give her his secrets as she gave away hers; following each others thoughts until they didn't need to think anymore; intertwined until he felt grief at the slightest separation; pride at Emily's decision to get herself an education; her struggle then her triumph in getting a degree and qualifying as a schoolteacher - a true vacation she adored, and a job by all accounts she was wonderfully good at. Looking back; looking forward, all struck Roux Surette at once as his eyes fell upon his wife and settled on no other - how lucky Roux Surette was; how Roux Surette was; how all, how all had fallen, into place.

XVII.

How Roux Surette was? It had burned Will Chaucer from the moment he saw Surette sitting in the darkest corner of Whites, looking back to an official document and forth to a large whisky, each engrossing the man to the exclusion of all else. Body language - expression; eyes; demeanour - the urge to react to the urge to take a look at the document Surette left on his table when he stepped onto Bourbon Street, was overwhelming.

Chaucer had seen the camera crews outside. He had guessed who they were looking for. This pre-occupied, evidently affluent and cerebral looking black man must have been an important fish in the New Orleans pond, judging by the amount of press and cameras that turned to focus upon him.

Reading the Preliminary Report, which described the execution of Darius Trémé, the answer was obvious as to why the press had found Roux Surette. Chaucer concerned himself with the detail - how it moved him; how it resonated, playing uneven chords, powerful discordances and destructive time. He contemplated his approach. How would he play at being himself; and how he would he play with Doctor Surette? There was only one way. He would seed and germinate an interest in a psychiatrist under pressure, and thus afford him some influence over Surette's analysis of Darius Trémé's killer.

The night, however, was for performance; for performance riddled with the memory of that dead child; of the murderer; of the suffering of both; of darkness and few shards of light; of punishment and astonishment; of astonishment; of creativity; and of the past.

The following morning and Chaucer had found the initial subterfuge easy to effect. The many psychiatrists of the past all had one thing in common - a pre-occupation with distortions of personality affecting capacity for judgement. This subjectivity and inherent self-interest precluded them from being definitive as naked interest - self-interest or not, erected barriers to true insight. The pre-occupation is all consuming; and the output the same - tangential analysis and enthusiasm bordering on obsession. Tedious. Surette would not and had not been capable of letting something slip from his grasp when there was potential to learn. And Surette had unknowingly assumed his role to perfection.

Chaucer had behaved like an apparently plaintive passenger in his own, his very own tick list of manipulation; and Surette acted and reacted precisely to all of Chaucer's thrusts and counter-thrusts the aim of which was to establish some sort of unbreakable interest-rapport with a commonplace man with an uncommonly large ego.

Surette's obsession had now enveloped him with an entirely understandable search for credibility. This particular fusion of pride, ego and arrogance, inherent in masculinity itself, was strong in Roux Surette. Chaucer did not, but should have anticipated Surette's insistence on credibility through the vagaries of his past through the search for knowledge, credibility and the need for pontification. When pontification came, Chaucer ignored it; for Surette was unknowing as to the truth and not Chaucer's myriad versions of the actuality.

Still, dredging the tangents of the past didn't come easy to him. What did he have to lose, for his English origins and the instabilities of his past were the very reason he had the ability to avoid the tragedies of the future. To unveil his history, would be worth the future. To have someone else poke and prod for matters in the past which may live as a predicator of the future, was a necessary elegy to make a dull man listen.

Surette had a choice. He would listen, or take the risk that he would tell the baying press of the true nature of the Trémé crime. The man had listened, true; the man was intrigued - but for how long; and how long before the death of another child?

It was eight forty five and Chaucer was about to play. He looked into Whites, straining his eyes to see the dark, abundant and shiny head of hair, which he presumed, represented the back of Emily Surette's head. It irked Chaucer that he couldn't see her face. Marital life - to Chaucer's face came a wry smile at the banality of expectation. Surette was a bore. A bore would choose a staid and correspondingly normal woman. Chaucer knew; and he wouldn't be holding his breath.

Chaucer surveyed the scattered and broken remnants of his life. Too often, he knew, people washed over existence and blamed the immediacy of the surroundings - the innate; the significant other, be it social or familial. He had chosen to look within, having been forced to look within. What an effort it had been to change the fundamental pivots of his personality. How strange for a nine year old to try; and desperate that a nine year old child should feel the need to run away from the urges bestowed upon him. Where did the drive to change come from? Why gift him the ability to denude and question desires to hurt and destroy? Why not just gift him the inability to question the pain he was capable of causing? Surely life would have been that much easier. Was reflective intelligence too much of a good thing? Clearly it could be if incessant analysis stopped him from ever following the clarity of the innate evil he had cornered inside. Why not let evil speak and follow a pre-ordained destiny? Why did he have to struggle on alone now? Why was Anna, his wife, not there to ameliorate the pain?

How he missed his wife. How he loved her. He was so lost; so, so, lost without the only person who understood him. He missed intimacy; he craved touch, warmth, care, kindness, understanding and the irreducible beauty of a fusion of minds at one in a desire to heed and bestow an unimpeachable love for each other. Sorrow weighed his heart. Sadness bullied his mind. Misery coloured his past. He missed Anna.

Chaucer thought of the last year. He thought of the reasons he came to New Orleans and of certain matters he had not explained to Roux Surette. Will Chaucer wondered whether Roux Surette would ask. Chaucer wondered whether he would tell him.

It was time to play. It was time to perform in front of an expectant and excited audience at Whites. Word of his talent had got round. Peeking from behind a curtain, Chaucer could make out the faces of half the New Orleans trumpet and jazz fraternity. The concentration of talent at the bar started curdling his guts, as he watched his trumpet playing heroes cajole and mock each other between throat sized doses of hard liquor.

Each had their own idea how to approach each of the standards he had chosen to play, for each of them would be able to mutate and deliver sounds comparable to those Chaucer would actually deliver on stage. And each would make mental notes, not on the basis of his technique, which was as good as any, but on his interpretation. Chaucer knew that he could dazzle most of the public audience with the pitch and intensity of his tone, and with the volume and the breadth of his range, but one thing he could not do was fool the cabal by the bar that technique and power represented anything other than a good jazz trumpeter and not an exceptional jazz trumpeter. That was what the night was all about. That was why the bar was rammed with New Orleans very finest. It was about acceptance. He would get gigs, cut records, be invited as a white Englishman into a fraternity far removed from Caucasian jazz. Acceptance tonight would make him; make all the early years; make all the pain and suffering he had endured as a child, entirely worth it. Because it all added up to this one evening and the one thing his talent needed - acceptance.

He needed a couple more minutes alone - somewhere quiet; somewhere to reflect; somewhere, to think. Anna. He closed his eyes and looked into hers. He heard the sound of her voice. He felt the softness of her skin. He would dedicate the evening to her. He would dedicate the evening to the struggles she had endured. He would dedicate the evening to his own father and the pain he had endured. He would dedicate the evening to himself.

Chaucer looked deep within. In his mind's eye, he looked at the rage in his stepmother's face the first time he was beaten and blood gushed from his nose. He looked at the faces of the children who attacked and maimed him when he was nine years old; at how they bared their teeth in unison, destroying him physically but resurrecting his mind. He looked at the face of the boy whose skull he had fractured and at the incredulity in that boy's eyes as he lay motionless in his hospital bed with bandages wrapped around his cracked skull - just looking at him - looking and searching for answers as to why he had done it - why?

Chaucer remembered the next few years. He remembered the endless beatings. He remembered fighting back and the further beatings which sometimes arose out of rage or alcohol, or plain hatred. Chaucer remembered the stress of being one man on the inside and learning to get along with the world by being another on the outside; and how he had managed to change and re-structure his personality over and above the hatred he was taught to portray; the anger he was taught to deliver and the violence he was supposed to mete out on all who got in his way. He thought of love, the concept of love. He thought of reliance. The same thought kept nagging his head. Nausea was enveloping his gut. How he missed his wife. How close he wanted to be to her. How he relied on her then and how he needed to rely on her now. Anna was the key to the evening. As tears fell and cascaded down Chaucer's face, as anger forced him into action, Will Chaucer climbed onto the stage of Whites, a man possessed by the past, and a man possessed.

If the audience had looked closely at Chaucer's face as he took a bow on stage, they would have seen these dull rivulets of tears falling down his cheeks. And they would have gained an overpowering impression of the depth of emotion Chaucer had summoned to express and alleviate his inner pain - salvation through sound; salvation through music; salvation, through jazz.

XVIII.

Surette looked at the audience. Several cliques seemed to have formed - a fraternity of jazz musicians at the bar - easy to spot, easy to ridicule; nearby a coterie of turgid money throwers there to be seen to be spending drug and crime dollars; and there were the others who he couldn't categorise - the miscellany; some of them alone and curious; some of them jazz fanatics who had heard of Chaucer's burgeoning reputation; some of them plain and immaterial.

Did he, belong? Being averse to the context made him unsure. It didn't matter; the music they were about to hear had little relevance and his natural antipathy was the output of a search for his destiny beyond the accepted parameters of Negro desire. Surette consoled himself - he was there to work; he was there, to work.

Chaucer looked gaunt; gaunt and somewhat misplaced when he stepped onto the stage. He looked shy and a little timid. Surette thought he saw a tear in Chaucer's eye. He asked Emily. She couldn't see one - that there wasn't a tear there. Chaucer tried to speak. But no noise came from is mouth. He seemed frozen; and the crowd tittered. Yet, the tittering crowd went unerringly quiet as Will Chaucer started his set with an old standard called 'Straight No Chaser.'

'Straight No Chaser' had a quick tempo and isn't a tune for those without the requisite technique to carry the standard off, let alone improvise over the top of its harmonic lines. Chaucer seemed to play with consummate ease, with fluttering fingers over the trumpet valves translating the vibrations of his lips, the thoughts in his head and according to Chaucer himself, the language of his heart. Even for Surette, an uninitiated man by his own admission, Chaucer invoked sheer awe at his technical mastery. The audience clapped spontaneously; enthusiastically. The naive clapped more than others.

His next standard was 'Summertime.' This is an old George Gershwin melody, from Porgy and Bess. Well chosen, Surette thought, for if he knew it, everybody else would know it too. Chaucer still looked tense. He looked distracted. Nerves can give justice to talent, Surette thought, or nerves can subtract from talent and claim talent for itself. How would justice treat Will Chaucer?

The answer was all around, for Chaucer played and improvised with such astounding clarity of line and rhythm and with such grace, embellishing Gershwin's soulful melody with note after note and phrase after phrase of undoubted beauty, that, as Surette looked and watched and analysed the faces of all of the people in the room, he knew it - he just, he just couldn't feel it.

People seemed to be in one of two places. Some just stared at Chaucer as he played; staring at the man's physical form trying to connect with the physicality of a human being who was reaching out to their essence - others, who had been smoking, let their cigarettes burn. All were transfixed either by Will Chaucer himself, or by their connections to a mental hinterland - Surette's poor description of the place between activity and thought during periods of self-contemplation.

Confirmation could be gleaned from the men at the bar - these self-professed jazz virtuosi. Chaucer had opened their eyes to the potentiality of music - to the potentiality that the trumpet had, if placed in perfect synthesis with a man such as the troubled Englishman who played to them, and with them. A face Surette recognised let a cigarette burn between his lips as Surette imagined him trying to work out how Chaucer was using the chord structures in the song and formulating patterns and sounds that belonged to a blend of maximal suffering and especial musicianship.

It was as if this man's playing made them travel - to the past; to the future in light of the past, or by exception to it. Where else would these people go due to the infection of the melancholic and utterly beautiful sounds which enveloped their ears and in turn, their minds? Where else were they going to go? They may well have travelled to the future but only to the future with reference to the mistakes and decisions they had made in the past.

Surette would say that Chaucer was infecting the heart, appealing to the heart and examining the heart, massaging the heart and calling to it to learn from the past and if not to learn from the past, to examine the past in light of the potential for the future. The man was lyrical - sometimes melancholic; still he raised the spirit or deflated it; and he examined all in that room for many reasons. The undoubted beauty of Will Chaucer's playing put together a collective psyche around Whites' stage that evening which was unique to the people privileged enough to be there.

Even Surette's wife, Emily, was, for want of a better word, smitten - she more than others as Surette could see her change under a range of emotions and seeming peculiarity of insight he, in all the time they had been together, had never seen before - emotions flashing across his wife's face as they travelled from her eyes and infused the muscles of her mouth and cheeks, while her cheeks intermittently flushed red and white and tears at times rolled down her face.

It seemed as if Chaucer had picked up something in Emily that Surette could not comprehend. Maybe Chaucer had managed to intrude into Emily's past. Maybe Chaucer's playing appealed to, touched and smothered emotions previously tinged but never plundered. It came as no surprise to see Emily look at Surette as Chaucer neared the end of the song, and extend her hand toward the hand of her husband, leaning over to him and telling him how much she loved him. Other couples in the room had done the same thing as the end of Chaucer's performance seemed to suggest a new beginning. But the moment didn't find Roux Surette. Most men would not have failed to be touched deeply by the moment and the outpouring of feelings in that room. For Roux Surette, the moment was lost.

When Chaucer had finished - finished his last note which he held on alone till all the air had been expelled through his trumpet, the room remained motionless and silence pervaded the air, perhaps for a minute, perhaps longer. The moment mattered to every person in that room, just as much as it meant to Will Chaucer himself, who seemed transfixed, his eyes closed for just as long as everybody there was transfixed by his magnetism and the sounds he had produced; until, finally, Chaucer opened his eyes and pulled his trumpet away from his lips. Then, only then, did the audience begin with a slow, tentative handclap which gradually broke out into applause laced with such gratitude and comments all around to partners, to companions and to strangers alike, speaking of the undeniable privilege of witnessing that performance of that song.

Emily Surette applauded so hard that Surette thought she would chafe the skin from the palms of her hands. She looked at Will Chaucer with complete adoration. That look made Surette jealous; it made him jealous of all that Will Chaucer was - whether the enigmatic man he first appeared to be that morning, the sensitive and deeply disturbed but brilliant man he appeared to be in the afternoon, or the most gifted performer of a musical genre Surette could not understand.

Surette often used to say to his patients - he said it so often that to him it became rather a cliché - life, he would say, is a series of decisions; and each decision is made from experience, but a great degree of decision-making is about taking experience and aligning it to intuition and perception. If one can put these together, one has a chance of making something positive happen.

He said this stuff because it obviated his responsibility to find definitive answers. Decisions would be put right back into the hands of the person he was advising and let him off the hook. And it wasn't even that Surette believed in whatever he had said. He didn't. He said it because it made life easier, and he liked the sound of his voice.

He could have said the same thing to Will Chaucer. Chaucer would have laughed. He could have relayed a whole litany of psychobabble and the man would have laughed right back in his face. Whatever he was, Will Chaucer was sophisticated and powerful - the question of just how strong this man was, put Roux Surette to the sword because it forced him to question who he was, and where he had come from.

Was Chaucer his nemesis; a true, nemesis; everything he could never be but wanted to be? How would he square the circle? How could he re-instate the ground between Will Chaucer's advancement since the morning, and his own withdrawal? Did Chaucer have an Achilles heal? Surette thought he had the answer. He would have the answer the following morning. He would have to live with his jealousy, and wait and see.

For the next two hours Chaucer held the audience - not a flicker, not an ounce of movement; so much so that at the end of the evening the bar manager was heard to complain that takings were down by half as no one had the time nor the inclination to buy any drinks.

Surette watched Emily, as her face and her expressions continually changed from enlightenment to enclosure to wonder. Surette felt surges of jealousy envelop him as he came to the steady realisation that what Chaucer had said of jazz earlier that day, with those rather flippant references to astonishment and the way music had the capacity to get under ones skin, could be seen in the faces of everybody in the audience, and especially in the face of his wife. Chaucer was right - the power of language is inadequate compared to the value of sound when transmitted as language but a language which bypasses the motor faculties of the brain and penetrates the darker recesses of experience itself.

What was power - the ability to command respect? The facility to make decisions? Certainly every time Chaucer made a decision, conscious or subconscious, to change a note, a phrase or a line, each was a decision of sorts, but to catch the heart and to infect the imagination. Surely this was the locus of power. What of that flautist leading unknowing children into the abyss? What was the Englishman leading them to - to the darker recesses of themselves? Chaucer's power came from his ability to have the audience taken to their own places to dwell, not to the same place, so one man's abyss could be another's enlightenment.

Surette offloaded ideas all day long to weak people. Chaucer's power was the indirect promotion of reflection rather than the direct power of suggestion - music, Surette could hear Chaucer saying, was not about forcing thought, it was about trying to inspire thought through the power of sound. Psychiatry had no such privileges. At worst it could be the hideousness of power in the hands of the vain and irresponsible; and at best, it could be a force for good only with the power of suggestion.

Did that make him any worse than Will Chaucer? Did it mean that in some hierarchy of worth, Chaucer was somewhere above him?

Surette hated the very idea. And he hated this new predilection for self-examination. Was Chaucer a better man than he? Absolutely, no. So why should this Englishman make him feel inferior? Chaucer was nothing superlative. Why did Chaucer make him feel uncomfortable? Why did Chaucer make him feel envious? Why, in fact, did Will Chaucer make him feel inferior at all?

XIX.

Reactions suggested excellence. The standing ovation was unprecedented, with four encores. Chaucer was quickly mobbed with his hand thrust into the palms of his heroes, and invited to jam and guest with them at their gigs as far way as New York and Chicago.

Chaucer was deeply touched. He had become a member of the 'brotherhood' as they called it - a vindication of his appeal to their suffering; to the suffering of black men covered in generational poverty and prejudice descending from the slave trade and man's inhumanity to man. The irony wasn't lost - happiness through recognition of mutual unhappiness, and he felt happy to oblige a celebration of the upside outcome of the downtrodden American majority.

When the moment had trickled by, savoured as it was; and most had left to the night, or to late night life in The Quarter, Chaucer's mind turned to Surette and his wife. He had one very particular recollection, namely that of looking down upon the faces of the Surettes and noting the differences in their demeanour - how Surette had eyes for the rest of the audience; that

Emily Surette was different - this wasn't the picture postcard American wife. She wasn't the blonde with the big hair and the bony backside American men like to parade. Emily Surette was simply dressed and elegant for it. She had long, thick black hair, smooth pale, milky white skin, full blood red lips and black - black eyes which contained little life if they contained life at all.

Chaucer found her off-putting; somehow distasteful - not because she did not feel the music - the tears in those eyes evidently told him that she was emotional; but those eyes, whether surrounded by tears or not, gave way not to depth, but to distance, like a profound but empty landscape; an oppressive landscape which revealed nothing except, nothing - no connections with anything meaningful at all; black and defined, but without definition. Similarly, she held a very distinctive aura - so inhibited and controlled yet her persona spoke of a deep sense of identity with his performance.

Chaucer now had clues as to how the Surette's marriage worked - Roux Surette was the emotional retard, relying on ego and flawed reason; Emily Surette was more emotional but to some degree, controlled. Was she prone, like Surette, to let her anger seep out now and again; to gravitate a little more from anxiety to delirium; prone to a little more humanity, yet still emotionally tight?

Chaucer approached them. He intended to speak to them as a couple, wanting to avoid the one-sided narrative he had engineered when in the company of Surette.

"Please don't stand up - not for a lowly Englishman. You must be Emily?"

Chaucer looked at Surette, then at his wife. He tried an eye smile. It didn't work.

"Thank you," she said, slowly, savouring every word.

"Thank you."

Surette butted in.

"Please; sit?"

Chaucer sat down. For a while he tried to indulge in chit chat. He tried; he failed. Chit chat wasn't Surette's thing and Emily Surette stared at Chaucer with doe-eyes, embarrassing her husband. Chaucer could sense her thinking, fantasising even, as could Roux Surette.

"You seem to have turned a corner in your career. They liked you."

"Well seemed is rather a woolly word. Maybe they did; maybe, they didn't."

Chaucer's mind was travelling; Emily Surette was beginning to make him fell uneasy. He felt, as she watched, that she was studying him; as if she were in a trance wrapping imagination around what she saw before her; but unconnected; distant; absent.

"What did you enjoy about tonight Mrs. Surette?"

Emily Surette had nothing to say or was summoning the right thing to say. Either way the minute was excruciating. Chaucer cut in.

"So did you like the slow tracks or the up tempo standards? I find it hard to decide myself. It rather depends on my mood."

"You play exquisitely. You, seem to understand. You really do seem to understand."

Such was the seductive nature of Emily Surette's delivery that Surette was full of shame. Yet it didn't seem to bother Emily as she closed her eyes and took a deep breath, unaware of the discomfort of her company. Surette apologised for her behaviour. Chaucer smiled.

"It seems as if I have something to say to your wife through music. Believe or not this happens with men too."

Surette stared hard at Will Chaucer. Chaucer sensed jealousy.

"Look; it has been a long day and I think I need to get some sleep."

Chaucer understood.

"Wonderful; you have provided us with a wonderful evening. If we could ever return the compliment we would only be too happy to have you over to our house for dinner one evening, when Roux isn't under so much pressure. It would be our pleasure."

"The offer is gratefully received. Unfortunately, I am going back to England the day after tomorrow"

Surette was taken by surprise. He had no idea Will Chaucer was leaving the United States. Surette tried to be diplomatic. Emily Surette pouted.

"Maybe next time you are in New Orleans then?"

Chaucer smiled; that smile again - the one Roux Surette was beginning to despise. Once the Surette's had left, and Chaucer made his excuses to the hangers on and the needy left at the bar, he stood outside, on Bourbon, and attempted to catch a cab. In the cooler night air, as the evening began to fall away, his thoughts began to stray, wandering and rambling into one another. At least The Quarter was quiet, he thought, although he doubted whether The Quarter has ever been quiet. Humanity and inhumanity in bed together - the good, the bad, the beautiful and all that is ugly. That is the French Quarter, he pondered; and that is, New Orleans.

Behind, the wooden doors of Whites unveiled a plain man. Chaucer exchanged glances with a nondescript male headed toward the residences in the south of The Quarter. A few seconds later, Bourbon Street was alive and The Quarter's quiet time was being punctured by the cumulative screams of police sirens.

Chaucer didn't know, but guessed that he had shared contact, for the first time, with Olivier Godin. Chaucer guessed correctly that Godin was heading in the direction of Chartres Street, no more than a mile away; heading toward another home in which there was the dismembered body of another child - this one a seven-year-old girl, who Will Chaucer would later know as Mia Laval. Chaucer did know, once again, that The Quarter was awake; that tragedy was in the air. Will Chaucer could only guess at what was to follow; and as quickly as the evening had embedded itself as triumph, the evening's triumph was redundant and forgotten as his imagination took him to the scene about to unfold no more than a mile away.

XX.

A dead weight pressed against Godin's stomach. He was contemplating what he was about to see. As blood-blind as the job had made him, experience had never eclipsed the sight of another dead body. Nerves and dread had enveloped and magnified to the point of nausea. Godin muttered a sombre greeting to the officers outside. No one returned the gesture.

"Godin; listen to me."

A police sergeant standing on the Laval's porch, spoke for all of them.

"Listen; you get the bastard that has done this. You get him. We don't care what you have to do or what you need; if you want help it is there. Any help - any help whatsoever."

Godin nodded. He was in no mood to object and wasn't going to object anyway. These were emotionally charged, tough men, who thought they had seen it all, and hadn't seen it all.

Godin was shown into the Laval's living room. Pat Kinnane, head of forensics with the New Orleans Police Department, a woman with six children of her own, was standing next to the body. Godin knew Kinnane well. Kinnane was originally from County Galway, in Ireland and had settled in the States when she was sixteen years of age, worked her way through school and earned the right to stay by her invaluable contributions to the community. Hard indeed Godin thought - hard and thoroughly honest.

"Olivier."

Godin didn't hear.

"Olivier; listen to me - listen. This is unholy. This, is the Devil's work."

Her last words had registered, albeit a couple of seconds after they were spoken. Godin was both transfixed and repulsed by what he saw before him. Kinnane's comments were almost trite, for what Olivier Godin had laid his eyes upon was in essence, evil and unholy. This was a child mutilated for simply being a child - an innocent child. Why take away the innocence? What purpose was there to taking away innocence? He asked Pat Kinnane to step outside. Godin couldn't talk to her with Mia Laval hanging not more than a yard away.

"My opinion, having seen both bodies, is that both of these kids were murdered and tortured in precisely the same way. I can see no substantive differences between the two bodies as both were severely beaten, had their tongues cut out, their intestines removed and burnt or simply cut, their limbs dislocated by the same pulley mechanism, the flesh pulled away from their limbs and boiling sulphur and wax poured into the clefts of flesh left behind; and both have had their little hearts cut out and slit while both were hung from the beams which traverse both this living room and the living room in Darius Trémé's house.

The only substantive difference I can see, is that after this little girl was killed, the killer then made the choice to cut off her head, crack open the skull and expose for show, or whatever this sick bastard intended, expose for the benefit of whoever found the poor little thing, the contents of the girls skull."

Godin asked why.

"Symbolism I think - show the contents of the head; show the physical contents of the head for what they physically are; show the brain and the epicentre of the victim's thoughts; define the personality; then eviscerate the child and detail the evisceration by exposing the redundancy of the mind to those who find the body.

That did not happen to Darius Trémé. With the boy, the message was different; whoever is doing this is using these children to evoke something of themselves, like an artist with a painting, or a composer with a score, the killer's medium of expression is the character of mutilation and the message that mutilation conveys."

Godin had heard enough to know, intuitively, that Kinnane was close. He had one more question. He asked about the note attached to Mia Laval's heart.

"The same idiotic verse as was left with the boy - the same pointless little verse exposing the twisted mind of an utterly evil man; no; less than a man - animals kill because they need to eat, but this monster kills because he needs performance."

Godin felt redundant. The killer had bolted and left the required amount of clues at the scene - not a clue more and not a clue less. The man was controlling the game. He had two more, important questions. Godin asked Pat Kinnane how long ago Mia Laval had been murdered; and how long the torture had taken to perform?

"Thirty minutes to an hour; maybe less - how long would it take to erect that array of madness? As to the time of death, my opinion currently, as we'll have to do some more tests, is that this killing took place late yesterday afternoon."

Godin left. As he walked up Chartres, Godin saw light several blocks north. Getting closer, he could make out the press and in front of the press, Roux Surette standing next to Eveny Brien. Unrecognised and part of a growing crowd, Godin heard Surette and Brien answering questions - the news was out; the sieve was leaking. Surette and Brien were public goods and the press were examining a man and a woman who were as much the victims as the dead children. Surette was squirming. Brien was composed.

Trying not to elicit enjoyment at Surette's evident demise, Godin slipped away, un-noticed and unscathed. The last thing he needed was a fetter upon his freedom to investigate the slim leads he did have. A low, almost non-existent profile was the source of power, and knew that Brién was purposefully standing in the way of the press. He thanked her for it.

Godin now had two weak leads - Will Chaucer and Surette's loose profile of the killer. Chaucer could not be considered until Godin had more information from Scotland Yard. As for Surette's offender profile, it had to some degree to be taken seriously, slim pickings or not.

Pat Kinnane called. A hurried autopsy had uncovered DNA evidence from the body of Mia Laval. Kinnane then explained that she had quickly had Darius Trémé re-examined, and found traces of the same on

Darius Trémé. It was a lead. Godin expressed his gratitude and made up his mind. He was going to eliminate people from the inquiry by obligatory mass DNA testing, using Surette's offender profile as the basis for choosing who would be forced to submit to sampling. If Surette was correct, the man who had perpetrated this crime was in there and was just one DNA test away from implication.

The unrest wouldn't matter. The death knell of his career was already being sounded and whether he snared the guilty or not, he would be pointing the finger of suspicion toward the powerful and the innocent. He had no choice. The selfishness and vanity of the powerful could not get in the way of retribution for the evisceration of the innocent. If it meant losing his job, so be it.

Godin walked home. His thoughts turned to his father. He checked his pager and saw that the hospital had not been in touch. He dreaded going back to their apartment. He considered going to the hospital. But he was very tired. He cursed himself for not being to stay awake, but knew his father would be at rest. And his mind was still full of what he had just seen. Anger pervaded him; and he needed to channel his anger through his grief. After a few hours rest, he would pound the street till the killer was caught. The sight of Mia Laval's body was all the preparation he needed.

Godin sifted through his pockets for his keys. Out of the darkness appeared two crumpled; two dishevelled, hunched silhouettes. Mia Laval's mother and father stood beside him. Kateri Laval was thumbing rosary beads. Their red, pleading eyes turned Godin's stomach more than the sight of Mia Laval's body itself. With a body, Godin knew what was coming next - that veil of objectivity he had once heard it called. But the image in front of was one of poor people with life draining their eyes, dead to all expectation. He tried to hold himself together.

They did not speak to him. Not a single word. As Godin prepared himself to offer utterly inadequate words of consolation, they stopped their silent prayer, looked at him and stared. And as much as he told himself it was a bad thing to stare back, Godin looked into the eyes of the little girl's parents and descended with them through pain and hideousness into an environment of loss and descending hopelessness wherein all enthusiasm for existence had left and all hope within the superstructure of human nature had been erased.

Godin's heart pounded within his chest. His felt slow and he was all but able to move. His mind had frozen to one thought in time and his constitution had been sapped of all but the utmost pity and despair at the sight of the decent, faithful and grievously wronged people standing in front of him.

How much faith; how much love must they have had in their hearts? How much love and faith they must have been able to give to their daughter and how much strength they had as Mia Laval's mother saw through the endless boundaries of her own grief and wiped away the tears from Olivier Godin's eyes?

Mia Laval's mother handed Olivier Godin her rosary beads. Godin's fingers closed over porous beads soaked with grief. How difficult it was for him to accept them. If he failed them now, Godin doubted whether he could handle to consequences. He watched them leave, heads bowed and arm in arm.

Olivier Godin went to bed; and dreamed - dreaming of being caught; of being trapped with no escape; wrapped around circumstances and feelings he could not control any longer; afraid he would somehow never be able to grasp the safety and comfort of the re-assurance of control; cast adrift from everything he had known; scared and vulnerable; tired and forlorn; without hope of getting back to the safer waters of the disciplines of the mind he once knew. He woke before his alarm and his bed sheets were soaked with sweat. And somehow his resolve and the wellsprings of courage which he had needed throughout his whole life were re-invigorated. Once more, he felt capable of taking on the evil which walked The Quarter.

XXI.

Surette couldn't sleep and couldn't dream - mixtures of images and questions; pictures and half baked conclusions colliding with and imploding within his glazing psyche - images of Darius Trémé; the image of Mia Laval's head severed from her body; Mia Laval's decapitated body drained of blood as it hung from a beam; an expression on Darius Trémé's face as his body dangled from a rope.

Why had these children been murdered? Murdered because they were innocent? Murdered because they had a future the killer had never had? Murdered because the killer had found his metier? Murdered because one man had unleashed the anger he had always controlled? Murdered because that anger had no other means of expression? Punishing the body for the sins of the mind?

Why was Mia Laval decapitated? Why was her head cracked open like a nut? What was the intention; what was the message in showing those who would find her, precisely that? Why was the same rhyme left by the side of the little girl's body? Why the same type of torture but a different conclusion? Why the need to exterminate life at all? Why children at all? Why attack innocence? Why was it always the innocent who suffered?

Surette sat up. Emily was fast asleep beside him. It was six thirty in the morning. He was exhausted; a mutating exhaustion creating negative energy redirecting analysis with a deep, searching and destructive agenda. In the solace of the night, when the iniquities of the previous day had set in and infected his moral order; after the sight, sound, touch and the stench of death had invaded and burned his nostrils; after his nemesis had arrived to finally pull down the curtain on his apparent acumen, Surette's half thoughts and reactions caught him descending toward this very particular bed of absolutes concerning himself. He glanced at Emily. He wanted to protect his wife and take care of his children. He needed to catch this killer and save his reputation. He needed to catch this killer to save the sanctity of the face he presented to his family.

Had he become a protectorate immediately or was it something he had always had within? Was the way he felt at six thirty that morning, on the back of several hours of mutating recollections; severe and twisted recollections of the perfidious nature of human nature itself; was he offering himself a knee-jerk and over emotional response to the gravity of the death of both Darius Trémé and Mia Laval?

The telephone rang.

"Doctor?"

Surette recognised the voice.

"I know; I've seen the news. But they haven't released details of what was found and what you have seen. Doctor; we must meet immediately. You must tell me precisely what you saw. In your office in one hour."

Chaucer hung up. Chaucer was plaguing his mind. Chaucer - but part of his life for less than twenty four hours, now a stamp of unyielding authority - he had no choice - Chaucer was commanding; Chaucer was now the integral part of the Trémé investigation. And he was an integral part of Surette's life - attractive to him because of the idiosyncrasies of his past and the uniqueness of his personality; attractive to his wife because of where his musicianship took her - places Surette could not allow her to go.

One hour. Surette got dressed and left. Chaucer was waiting for him at the clinic on Royal. Luckily, the press weren't. Unknown to either, Godin was sitting in the coffee shop opposite. Greetings were muted.

"My certainty Doctor; my absolute certainty, is that the killer is very close to the families of both Darius Trémé and Mia Laval. Only someone known to the killer and if my supposition is right, thought of as harmless to the local police, is the perpetrator of these killings."

Surette wasn't listening. Obsession; his search for answers precluded him from making a definitive decision on the subject. He wanted Chaucer to finish telling him the story of his life up until the point he departed England.

"Doctor; this is absolutely; absolutely unhealthy. Two children lie cold upon a slab and all you want to know about is what happened to me before I came to this town? Did I not prove it to you yesterday?

Understand; we are not one and the same; and we never can be. Some minds float in the ether while some trundle haplessly along the ground. We are the product of difference; and you cannot be that which you are not. What is past is past and losing value fast now that another child has been murdered. This issue of my past allowing you to embellish your future is getting in the way of finding a killer. Doctor; who do you think you are?"

Surette bit his lip. He had never been spoken to so cruelly; had his integrity questioned and his judgement pricked; and never before had he felt so childishly stubborn. He wanted Will Chaucer to continue; he would have a pound of Will Chaucer's flesh. And Will Chaucer would have to earn the right to give a pound of his flesh, whether Will Chaucer liked it or not.

"Alright Doctor; alright. You win. Today you win. Why you should want to continue the contest between reason and emotion, which is a conflict that surfaces ever more so, is mystifying quite apart from being horrifically selfish. I seem to bring out the worst in you."

Patronising; Chaucer indulging him - he wasn't; Surette knew that he, was indulging Chaucer, no matter what Chaucer thought. But Chaucer was right - he did want to know more and more - how Chaucer had explained the violence of his earlier life; how he purposely changed his personality and so questioned every single native emotion he had had subsequently and set about making those emotions accord with the prevailing values of the social world; how he had changed to fit in; how evidently Chaucer despised what he innately was. Chaucer had described school and his affinity with music; that his ability to play had won him a place at a prestigious school; the difficulty in fitting in and how he had come to know one of his fellow pupils with whom he had recognised the mutual affects of child abuse; how they had seen in each other the traits following naturally from the environments both of them had suffered at the expense of their parents; how they came close to each other, in a mutual world of understanding; how they had come to have feelings for each other which commenced with shared secrets and the journey to reliance.

"Forgive me Doctor; I am not so sure I can continue from were I left off."

Surette explained that Chaucer and Anna had come to spend more and more time together, in secret.

"Yes; of course. You have to imagine a school of such tiny proportions; a tiny school of rumour and counter-rumour. Imagine how difficult it was to be by ourselves. Everyone wanted to know Anna because Anna was so gloriously beautiful and mysterious. With forty young men chasing any woman with a pulse, let alone one like Anna who could stop traffic, you have to imagine that the scrutiny was pervasive.

But we had our meeting places. You remember how I told you how we first exchanged words - just simple words in the library with me going first and Anna too shy to deliver even the simplest of greetings."

Surette asked why.

"Sometimes it takes one victim to recognise another. Do you remember? I had previously conquered the urgent to use violence, or wholly sublimated it, and what fell out of the other side was a quiet boy sitting on top of the execrable drivers of my personality. Such conflict gives off an odour; and others can smell it. Anna was different of course, with her background driving her method, as Anna shied away from all attentions of the opposite sex, without exception."

Surette asked Chaucer to describe his physical appearance.

"Physically, I was very much I think as you see me now. I have always been rather boyish; rather young looking. I can remember people mistakenly believing I was a girl. I still bear freckles across the bridge of my nose, even today."

Surette understood - Anna felt uncomfortable with men who were older; she felt comfortable with Chaucer because he was unthreatening.

"These things have more subtlety and complication than that. Perhaps I am not getting my point across; maybe I am but you cannot understand it. Maybe matters are difficult when one is picking out the past when it is so obviously riddled with feelings."

Surette assured Chaucer and for once, felt a little on top. Surette was now certain - it was to do with how these two teenagers grew together; what happened when they first started to explain deeper feelings and experiences to each other. Sacred ground.

"It took a long time; a long time and after we had left school. We moved to London. We lived separately with acquaintances. We lived separate lives. We stayed very close; and together, we retained our secret."

What, secret? Was this a platonic friendship of the kindred; or had it flourished?

"We were best friends; we were intellectually intimate; but we did not disclose to each other for almost two years. Recall Doctor; men who retard their character live under restriction and I did not have the facility to look at the opposite sex. Anna was really the only person I could relate to and the only person I wanted to relate to.

Still, I must say, London was good to both of us. As a child, Anna had been isolated from life's practicalities - me, too; and we were both shy and insecure, so London helped us grow as we were forced to come out a bit; to unveil ourselves and to undertake what for most, are the simple things in life. Shyness is an awful thing. Marry shyness to repression, and the inner connectivities within a young and fragile character are going to be tender. Enjoin shyness, repression and systematic psychological abuse and one may have an insidious cocktail likely to destroy the faculties of human expression the rest of us take for granted. London was good for both of us. If we hadn't spoken, we would have gone under. But we didn't."

Surette asked how and when they spent time together.

"Mostly weekends - Anna and I lived a few miles apart. I would generally go over to where Anna lived, in a gorgeous flat overlooking the River Thames. We would spend our weekends alone. Anna did find it difficult to make friends. London can be an acutely difficult place to make friends; an acutely lonely place. Our weekends were spent with each other. We would go for walks in Greenwich Park, visit Art Galleries and go to concerts."

What of Anna's beauty?

"Oh; incredibly difficult - incredibly difficult. We could be taking a walk in Greenwich Park and men would stop playing football just to look at her; I remember once taking her to the pub and having to take her home due to the attention. No; Anna's beauty was an enormous problem for her."

Surette feigned a lack of understanding. Annoyance flashed across Chaucer's face.

"A world were you are vaunted for your face and your body; looked at everywhere you go; stared at; scrutinised; where one has women call you a bitch for no other reason than the shape of your body and the character of your face; people assuming you are better, brighter, more charismatic, wealthier, luckier and likely to get exactly what you want, when you want it and how you want it, just because you are pretty.

Many times would we walk past women, young or old, pretty or not, who would say something utterly vindictive or nasty about Anna's appearance. How many men would pass their sly comments to Anna as to why she shouldn't be with someone like me; how they would be better for her; how their shoulders were broader and protection was assured - laughable, risible, plain poor."

Surette suggested that appearance was at the epicentre of want. He noted of the lack of logic in that Chaucer could vaunt Anna's beauty, then criticise others for reacting to it.

"There are many arguments about the virtues of physical beauty. Anna's real beauty was within. Exteriors are for the fickle and myopic. There are a million people out there who want to be vaunted on the basis of their physical features, sad though that is. What is more illogical than a society which pedestals beauty then punishes the beautiful?"

Surette cut to the chase. Chaucer looked incredulous.

"Oh of course we fell in love. We had no one else. All we ever were to each other was all we ever had."

And music?

"I began to despise formal music. The music of the dead - Chopin, Liszt, Brahms and all of the others, had little to offer me anymore. Formal play is about scales of imitation - the most meaningful imitations of the wiles of someone else. Jazz; sorry, improvisation, is about me. The trumpet was something I could express myself through, and it became increasingly apparent to both of us that in order to have a fruitful life together I would have to drop formal music instruction and go back to university - which I did."

The admission that he studied law at Oxford - but jazz; but music?

"More of a hobby then; more of an obsession now."

Chaucer began life at Oxford?

"Yes I did. And a thoroughly miserable time for the both of us it was too, at least, initially. Anna and I spent the first year apart. Eventually she got a job in Oxford as a violin teacher. And the law course was going to be useful from the perspective of getting a job at the end of it, or staying in academia.

Oxford was good to me. I enjoyed having the freedom and through private reading I understood more. With each passing day I felt a greater confidence about being just a normal person in public, notwithstanding the litany of psychological problems dwelling behind my eyes."

Tedious; little by way of substantive detail in this historical exposition; and Surette was disinterested. He wanted intimate details - the idiosyncrasies of shy people are one thing, but Chaucer had reported little as to how these tendentious psychological maladies were resolved.

Incongruence; Chaucer had portrayed himself as an extremely strong character; Surette had to admit that he was, a particularly strong character, but that didn't tally - shyness can be indicative of insecurity.

"All I need to do is explain meanings behind tangents that do not tally with conformist views, proving to you that I am qualified to profile both the killer of Darius Trémé and now, sadly, Mia Laval. A shy disposition is irrelevant. But you can see how it complicates matters - shy people often invert and fall into imagination and creativity given that the social world can be a forbidden place.

It seems to me is that all you are interested in is how I resolved matters of a physical nature with Anna. If I am candid on these matters which are close to my heart, then I will be giving an exposition of such detail that I will not be edifying nor will I be nice. But you will have all you crave."

"When, as I said, I went to Oxford, Anna followed and we decided for the first time we should live together. It was the practical thing to do. For the years we had been best friends; for all the years we had shared each other happily to the exclusion of everybody else, the most we had ever done, was kiss; was to look at each attempting to express how we felt without ever saying it. In time, as we grew to love Oxford; as she grew into her job and we grew out of the parameters of repression that had brought us together, we grew stronger."

"One day we went walking in Snowdonia, which is a mountain range in Wales. We climbed all day and reached the summit absolutely exhausted and alone, looking out across a landscape of mountains and rain soaked valleys. And in that solitude, hand in hand, looking into the distance on a beautifully clear day, I turned to Anna and asked her to marry me."

Chaucer smiled.

"And do you know what she said?"

Chaucer grinned.

"She said yes; she said, yes."

Surette referred to the marriage. Chaucer's countenance changed. Pleasure was immediately circumvented by pain.

"We did get married. And it was a very, very private affair. Only our best man and Anna's maids of honour, who were a couple of her violin pupils - older women, attended."

A church?

"We are Roman Catholics and got married in Roman Catholic Church."

And the service?

"We kept the wedding as secret as possible. As far as we were aware it was between us and that was that. It was our day and our life we were considering. Unfortunately it did not turn out like that."

Chaucer's countenance became black.

"After we had undertaken the vows and the priest had said the blessing, we turned to leave, only for Anna to see a man I soon understood to be her father."

Surette sensed he was getting close.

"Anna's father turned up our wedding day - the happiest day of Anna's life, now ruined by the appearance of - and to this day we do not know how he found out that we were getting married - of that evil, insidious bastard.

Anna saw him and ran. And I mean, ran. And the man stood there, at the back of the church, with his arms out waiting to be hugged. I, of course, went after her.

Later, I learned from the priest that Anna's father began laughing once Anna had fled. He was still laughing when he got into his car and drove back to wherever the fuck that miserable bastard came from.

I found my wife Doctor, still crying an hour later, cast in foetal position, underneath a tree in an adjacent park, with her thumb in her mouth, rocking backward and forth. She didn't recognise me at first, and when she did, she backed away - didn't want me to go near her at all; didn't want the one man she had loved and the man she had just got married to, to touch her; to help. This poor, lost soul was trapped in the present by the prettiness of her face and trapped in the past by the insidiousness of the cruel man who had turned up at the church on our wedding day."

Surette now saw it as a matter of outcome.

"Eventually, Anna came round and let me take her back to our home, where we had prepared a little food and wine for the few guests we could count as friends. They had left by the time we got there. So there we were - Anna and I - alone, looking at each other, searching for those re-assurances that kept us as close as you could ever possibly imagine and unable to so speak save to just sit together - the best day of our life ruined; the most important day of our life ruined, until something inside me snapped; something snapped Doctor and all of the anger I had stored for all of those years, came out in this, our weakest moment. I began talking to my wife explicitly. Yes Doctor - explicitly - that very afternoon."

How did Anna take the suggestion?

"Frightened; unsure; trapped; vulnerable. I went first. We held hands and sat on our bed; Anna still in her wedding dress and me still in a morning suit; and I told her everything in explicit detail - all I had experienced during the course of what passed as a childhood, showing her the scar tissues all over my back and why that had happened."

What of Anna?

"I spent two and a half hours telling Anna everything - the violence and my responses to it; how I was beaten; that I was taught to hurt; how the psychology of destruction and evisceration was planted and germinated inside my head - the head of a small child. Everything - that I tried to hurt people; how one day they turned on me and how I fractured that boy's skull; urges I could never discard; the proclivities of violence which consumed my inner self; and how I learnt to replace them. I told Anna how I was less than a human being, more a pre-programmed machine designed to react in order to retain acceptance and not rejection. Two and a half hours to encompass a lifetime of repression Doctor - not bad really.

To this day I feel meek and duly humbled as I sat for the rest of the day listening to what Anna told me of the man who had ruined our Wedding Day. See then it was Anna's turn. It was Anna's turn to break down the final barrier and like me she said she wanted to start at the beginning. I tried to hold her hand but she brushed me away.

It took her twenty minutes to say anything. All of the time she kept her gaze firmly fixed on mine; looking at me into me and through me, trying, even after all our years together, to see if she really could tell me and believe in me, which she undoubtedly could.

It first happened when she was seven years old. Anna's mother worked as a night school teacher several evenings a week, as they needed a little extra money. Normally, upon returning home, Anna's mother would run a bath for Anna before she went to bed. However, given that Anna's mother was out, it fell to Anna's father to do the same - something Anna said she felt entirely comfortable with. Why shouldn't she?

However, Anna's father started by insisting on watching Anna undress while he sat on a chair opposite. He insisted that she bathe herself - something she had not done before, while he stared. He then had her bathe herself with her legs open, facing him. Then he asked Anna if they would like to play a private game - something between the two of them and something they must keep between themselves. He put his hand into the bath water and rubbed his fingers against her."

Surette looked at Chaucer's face, searching. He found, impassivity. Surette had read accounts similar to this before, but never had he come so close.

"Now I have tried to seek a kind of forgiveness for what that man did next. But I cannot forgive him for what he did because not only did he penetrate my wife's body, he made the choice to play, mutate and desecrate Anna's mind from the moment he started trying to get Anna to please him and assuage his guilt by having her tell him how much she liked what he was doing."

Surette asked what happened next.

"After a few occasions, he realised that Anna knew that his behaviour was wrong, so he began what I now understand to be a common tactic amongst paedophiles - emotional blackmail; the conscious manipulation of Anna's mind so that guilt would be transposed to her should his sick and incalculably evil behaviour become known."

Surette wondered if it got worse.

"That first occasion was just the beginning. Several months later, Anna made the choice to bathe herself and locked the bathroom door behind her. Her father broke down the door and ordered her to repeat what had been done a few months previously."

Surette could see Chaucer change - more intense; his voice stronger, powerful; more focused. As Will Chaucer reached the focal point of his response, the white's of his teeth began to show, like a feral carnivore.

"Anna believed her father's threats as to what would happen to her if she told another soul. He told her she would be killed if she spoke; and he began threatening her with her life if she breathed a word of what he was doing."

Surette asked Chaucer if Anna described how and whether her personality changed. The question angered Chaucer. Surette berated his own stupidity.

"What do you think, Doctor? You have a normal happy and well-adjusted child, a sociable child and a child disinclined to be any bother. Within a few months you have a child being psychologically and sexually abused by a father she had only previously had adoration for. Of course that affected her."

Surette took the admonishment graciously. What about Anna's mother?

"She had no idea and still has no idea to this day what her husband did to her only child. Anna never told her. Anna knew it would have killed her."

Did Anna's mother ever realise?

"Anna started to withdraw; she stopped being sociable at school; she became introspective and morose; and she would avoid situations at home where her father was in and her mother was out. Still, Anna's mother did not know, even when comments were made at Anna's school as to the fairly evident changes in her personality.

You see you have to remember, at the time, in England, little sinister was suspected in these changes. Child abuse was something ill understood and a matter more likely not to be suspected than the converse. When something like that is not on the tips of parental acumen and the consciousness of teachers, it was probably the last thing to be considered. If you have someone as scared as Anna was - literally in fear of her life - ask yourself, is she going to speak out? Would you speak out? She was just one small, insignificant child in an aggressive adult's world without the courage to speak for fear of being dismissed and thrown right back into the perfidious arms of her father.

Besides, as his behaviour got worse, so did his threats. The man seemed to enjoy the destruction of his only child. He would wake her up about an hour after she had gone to bed and put his hand down the front of her pyjamas, asking her if she liked it. On the occasions when Anna had the courage to say no, the man would get worse; hideous; un-Godly."

Surette was repulsed. Chaucer seemed to sense it.

That was enough. That was definitely enough.

"That is definitely not enough," Chaucer shouted as his voice and his whole persona brimmed with anger.

"That is most definitely not enough Doctor. It is not enough, no matter how grotesque Doctor, because it is not all I have to say. He did not end there. You must be told because you asked; and you must be told because this actually happened and this actually happened to my wife."

Tears started forming in Will Chaucer's eyes. His chin began to shake. His voice began to quiver.

"That bastard Doctor; that bastard took my Anna one night several months later and raped his only daughter."

Now Doctor; is that, enough?"

Surette had heard more that he had ever needed to hear. His stomach churned over and over again. Surette was not only saddened by this man's story, he was sad for himself; he was concerned for himself and he was concerned for all parents and more particularly children who at that moment had to endure the same hideous punishment just for being a child.

He spent some considerable time in silence. He needed to compose himself. Looking at Chaucer, he knew that Chaucer needed the time to compose himself too, for Will Chaucer was sitting on the end of Roux Surette's couch with his head in his hands, looking toward the floor. But

Chaucer still seemed to want to keep talking. He seemed to have plenty more to say.

"I have suffered in my life for what was done to me in the name of a twisted desire to do what my stepmother considered was for the best. Compared to Anna I have not suffered at all. Sure I bear physical and mental scars for all that was done to me. But they are nothing compared to what my wife had to walk around with in her head every single nanosecond of every minute of every day of her life.

Not only was she hideously sexually abused; but when she grew into a woman she was so pretty that the one thing which had destroyed her - sexual abuse; sex; male manipulation and deceit, resided in the face and in the actions of every single male she ever came across. Every catcall, jeer, insinuation and come-on had Anna recoil in horror, and when she had to deal with an older man, especially those who looked at her sexually, she felt the need to crawl up into a little ball and cry. And as Anna told me on our Wedding Day, just like all she did thereafter, she asked herself the simple question - why; why her; why was she treated so badly? Just - why?

Can you see now why we found each other? Can you see how both Anna and I were two of a kind? Can you not see how it is so easy to destroy a child while they are still alive? Can you not see what a responsibility it is to bring a child into this world? Can you not see how important it is to be a good parent? Can you not see how, for want of a better description, the metamorphosis of children creates a disjointed and cruel world? Can you not see how cruelty manifests itself in the adult before the child? Can you not see how precious children are? Can you now believe how east it is to kill that innocence if one has had that innocence so cruelly taken away?"

Roux Surette had now heard enough; had been sufficiently moved by Will Chaucer and had seen enough of Chaucer's insides to know that here was an entirely genuine man. And here was a man who cared, not just for the woman he loved but for the lives of all souls who had had their freedom and innocence taken away.

As far as Surette was concerned, Chaucer was unique, for he had never met nor read of, interviewed or counselled anybody who had the same depth, emotional intelligence, and sense of morality; and, the same and hideously shifting sands underneath upon which it was all based. Here was a man worthy of the emotion of jealously and admiration. Surette realised that there was no shame in feeling jealous; and proud; and arrogant, in front of a man with this personality. Surette knew he was not the same; Surette also knew that he couldn't compete. Will Chaucer was right; right at the very beginning - he had the one thing Roux Surette had not - experience.

A final question remained unresolved.

What had happened to Will Chaucer's wife?

XXII.

All Godin had was his past; bits of his future - a man with no past until Scotland Yard got back in touch; and a man with a limited future given the return ticket to London. Being unaccounted for when Mia Laval was murdered meant nothing under the law - there was to be no arrest without substantive reason; and suspicion without reason was not enough reason.

Godin could still have Chaucer tailed, and did so. And at some point that very morning or in the early afternoon Godin would have a thorough and hopefully penetrating analysis of William Chaucer - schooling; family; criminality; history. Godin had seen at first hand how easily the British could settle a big brotherly eye upon their supposedly free subjects. The return would be thorough. But would it be enough?

Godin turned to the only other lines of inquiry - the DNA evidence identified by Pat Kinnane; and Surette's only substantive point to date - that the blood rhyme indicated that the killer knew Darius Trémé and Mia

Laval. He called his team together. He told them to collect the names of all peoples known to the Trémé and Laval family. All of the males were to provide DNA to compare their genetic material with what was left at the crime scenes. There would be no exceptions. He returned to his office and looked at the blood rhyme once more.

"They say a great deal of success often comes down to happenstance. Luck, I think, is one of preparation's natural oversights. How, after all, can one prepare for definition when life is a collection of so many coincidences?"

Godin looked up. He tried to stand. She asked him not to.

"One can create circumstances in which luck can prevail. One can manipulate odds and circumstances will manipulate outcomes; whether the outcome is the right one depends on the circumstances."

Eveny Brien smiled. Godin wondered why she was being so obscure.

"For all of the efforts of your men, I believe you will have little chance of identifying a suspect. It is good old fashioned police work and must be done. You handled them really well seeing as none of them wants to work for you."

Godin hadn't considered his isolation, not yet, that morning. He disliked Brien for bringing it up; for poking fun at him.

"Come; I am not being serious. They have a job to do now and must do it. Now, what are you are going to do; and how I am going to help you. The bunker you reside in is deep enough already."

Godin thought he heard a little contrition and dare he think it, a little humanity. He considered her motives as she made herself comfortable. Brien looked Godin in the eye and spoke simply. Pretence; arrogance and protections, had seemingly, been disregarded.

"When I first started this job, I was full of virtue and good intentions. I had a vocation and to put it loosely, I wanted to help. The police force seemed a natural choice. One Saturday afternoon, when I was twelve years old, I was staying at my Grandmother's house in on Governor Nicholls Street, just off Bourbon. I saw an ambulance pull up, next door, and a young boy with a compound fracture of his arm being carried, screaming, to an ambulance. A police car arrived and escorted the ambulance to the hospital. I knew that boy and could see just how much pain he was in. I wanted to be an ambulance driver at the time because those good people took that boy away to be treated. But I also remember the return of that police officer, after he had stopped the traffic in order to let the ambulance get to hospital quickly. I remember him particularly because I went next door with my Grandmother to console her neighbours. And I remembered the kind and gentle words that man said, as he commiserated with the boy's family. I remembered how compassionate he was and thought of how he didn't need to be there, nor did he have to speak the way he did. He helped them. He was kind to them. He saw them through the first few hours of a horrendous situation. And his kindness inspired me. From that moment on I decided that I too wanted to help people; to stop the causes of pain; to help create and maintain a society in which concern for others and showing others how to behave was paramount. I would remember that officer's face if I saw him now and I would like to thank him for giving meaning to the life of a little girl."

Brien paused. When she spoke she seemed to choose her words carefully.

"The police officer, who came to our neighbour's help that day, was Jack Godin - your father. And the face of that man is looking at me right now - you, Olivier, are worthy to follow in your father's footsteps. Some of us, alas, are not."

Godin felt sorrow and pride well up within; then, distraction. Why tell him that story - why? He felt himself drifting for his cynicism had deep roots yet a deal of him wanted to unfetter the responsibility of isolation. But something wouldn't allow him. She was trying to draw him out, but safety within was the veil outside.

"I, too, look at the police force as an honourable profession. In my opinion, for what it is worth, I will always believe that it is. I believe that a lot of your colleagues feel the same way. Not everyone is as strong as you. Human beings live together not because they have strength in numbers and can ward off attack - those primeval days are over; no - we have got used to being together without having to look over our shoulders in the way we used to. Hence, we have no sense of togetherness. When there isn't the enemy there to see, enabling us all to fall in together, we don't fall in together and we fight amongst ourselves. Crime is not the enemy in this office, nor is it the enemy in this country - crime is the ugly face of the economic freedom and liberal nature of the system of governance we adopted when this country was fashioned; and crime is acceptable because we expect it and most want for it as a marker between us and them - the good and the bad; compassion and monstrosity; right and wrong. To commit crime is expected and if expected, never questioned. We accept crime as read and we never challenge its roots. And we have become hardened to the wider questions because they are small bolts in an engine the sheer size of which overwhelms us. We catch those who commit; the perpetrators commit again and we catch. That is it.

So what happens to our society? The primeval need for togetherness is still strong even if the societal imperative is weak. So; what else - we look inward; we look in here. We search for differences amongst the group. And the search for differences and the need to belong puts inordinate pressure upon us all to be the same; to think the same; to act the same; to unveil the same prejudices; to follow the common denominator for fear of standing out and being banished.

I, too, have been guilty in my career of doing the same thing. It takes an extraordinary amount of bravery to swim against a tide as strong as the collective will. For those who don't follow the rules there is the indignity of excommunication no matter how, over time, those rules are skewed and mangled. As I sit in front of you now, no doubt explaining matters in a convoluted way, I want you to understand - all around you are weak men; and I too, am weak. But I can make a difference because I grasp the mentality of the mob. I have to manipulate the mob to get them to work for me. I know you are very close to your father. I know that he is the only conduit you have. You must believe me when I tell you I am on your side. You must believe me.

I want you now to look at me, not as Chief Eveny Brien - what is in a title? They are just inroads for the meek to deify. I can see through the façade - the very real façade of this environment. Forgive me for not respecting your integrity when we first met. Please, indulge me with your concerns with regard to this terribly diseased man who has infected The French Quarter. Please, be secure that I am beyond the petty vices of those who wish to see you fail. All I wish for is for you to succeed. Indulge me with your feelings; you have not lost the desire to help; you are kind, gentle and compassionate - just like your father, so you should not look up to me but tell me all you think as an equal. Please; make this particular Chief of

Police believe that once again she has the idealism you convey and let her feel the resolve to serve which your father gave me all those years ago, when I was a little girl."

Godin couldn't identify what words were on the tip of his tongue. He had no idea where those words would go. As close as he was to believing her, the more he wanted to pull away. She had invaded his private domain. He was an outsider. Isolation from the collective psyche is always an effective bar to assimilation with others. He depended on isolation. The more he cut his feelings off from others all the more deeply into self-dependence would he fall. And the deeper he fell the harder it would be to ascend and begin to trust. Life behind the veils of persona, as those veils got thicker, saw the persona take over. He knew; the first words of sincerity to depart his mouth would open the floodgates to harm, with the potential to destroy all he had built within as he tried to come to terms with his feelings, sexuality, moral outlook and the urge to serve.

"You are very kind about my father."

"He was very kind to me."

"I shall tell him all you have said."

"I would rather you tell yourself that I am sincere. Integrity is so hard to come by. I believe in yours. I beg you, please believe in mine."

XXIII.

The knock was distracting - weak; a percussive timidity suggesting reluctance; nerves, even. It was probably Quinn. This seeming timidity remained at the door, but behind it. Suddenly, Chaucer came alive, and pulled the door as hard as he could. Emily Surette was standing on the other side.

Her eyes caught Chaucer first - he had forgotten just how hopelessly black they were; how bottomless they seemed - eyes punctuated by a milk white complexion; a perfect milk white complexion surrounding contrsted with those vast pits of blackness beyond which lay the mind of Emily Surette. Grace too; as Emily Surette glided past him without averting her gaze, kissing her husband on the cheek.

Grace; she had the same grace he had seen in Anna - the same fluidity of movement; the same calmness of response to her environment; the same sense of stillness and serene reassurance which Anna had exuded. The likeness was remarkable in many ways. They were both tall. Height helped with estimations of grace, as did the fact that both Anna and Emily

Surette were slender and lithe. But Emily Surette was dark and Anna's hair was as blonde as sunlight.

Chaucer let these impressions pass him by. But he couldn't evade the idea that last night and at that very moment, he was being watched.

"Roux and...."

Emily looked at Chaucer, not knowing what to call him.

"Will; I hope you don't mind me being intrusive like this. I don't get the chance to see my husband that often these days"

Over the years, Surette had had never known Emily to come to his practise during the course of a working day; and she had never shown any sort of personal interest in his profession at all.

"Have you ever heard a man play an instrument like that before?"

Surette's discomfort was obvious.

"I have never been so touched so deeply by one man's playing. I shed tears during your performance."

The stillness; the certainty of delivery and control that emanated from Emily Surette made Chaucer uncomfortable."

"Gentlemen; please – this silence is uncomfortable."

"So you enjoyed last night Mrs Surette; you enjoyed my set? It must be very difficult for you at the moment to sit through anything; to see anything in straight lines when you have lost two children so close to your own little boys?"

"I enjoyed last night more than anything I can remember. You seem to have a way; something about the way you approach sound itself, which had the impression upon me of, well for want of a better word, of astounding me. You are so lucky. You are so lucky knowing that you can have that effect on people and please you own very sense of self. I wonder where it comes from; and why you would need to sit on my husband's couch and talk to him. It doesn't seem as if you could learn anything here."

If Surette took offence, Chaucer couldn't see it. There was insight in this woman - more insight than her self-serving husband. There were the references to how he had touched others; the idea of astonishment; self-perceptions - reflections of how the music pleased his 'very own sense of self.' How did this woman see so much?

Roux Surette was preoccupied, and focused on why his wife was deflecting his concerns. Two of her pupils were dead; and Emily was awash with Chaucer. Before Emily had heard Chaucer play, Emily had shown such sorrow. Now she seemed willing to push the tragedy away like a table of unwanted liquor.

"Presumably school is as sad as you could ever imagine. How are the kids taking it?"

Chaucer saw that Emily Surette was aeons away, floating in some self-designated hinterland located between reality and her rather peculiar flirtations and impression garnering.

"I'd rather not talk about it. It seems as if it is the only topic of discussion here. I can hardly get out of the school gates without being accosted by one reporter or another."

Chaucer tried to pursue the conversation. Emily butted in.

"Children being what they are, we don't see them as being too badly affected by the detail which has emerged in the local press. The mind of a child is not equipped to deal with the nature of these crimes. The mind of a child needs nurturing and attention when it comes to the nature of grief and loss. But children are far more resilient than one may think."

Emily Surette put on her jacket. Her demeanour changed again - she stood still; upright; motionless; and taught. She faced Will Chaucer, her square shoulders facing his - looking at him; through him; penetrating everything about him; trying to establish meaning; establish some sort of reference; a reason. Then she smiled; her eyes twinkling; an attractive smile; a smile of friendship; almost a smile of kinship.

"You know, in my experience as a teacher, Mr Chaucer, people assume it is easy to imagine what children feel and what children think - adults especially. But adults approach the subject from a peculiarly adult point of view; and I have learnt through the years, to respect a child's mind for what it is; and not how it can be changed to fit into an adult world. To do that risks taking that innocence in all children which is we should cherish and preserve.

One child grieving for the demise of another is a process for children to endure alone. As with all matters relating to kids, trying to change them when one doesn't understand them can only have disastrous consequences. So they grieve in their way and I grieve with them. My only prayer is that they haven't lost their innocence too, because innocence is the last vestige of virtue; and we live in a virtue less world. Questions and reasons and causation, Mr Chaucer; what if the world were a simpler place, and we could all, understand, all? Questions, and reasons, and causation."

XXIV.

Godin was getting nowhere. All his men were doing was a basic mathematical exercise in reducing numbers and verifying the alibis of the wealthy and connected. Potential suspects, were numerous. Some of them were absurd. Surette himself was a suspect; so was the Mayor of New Orleans. There were a total of forty names to go on; forty DNA samples to collect; forty to the power of all their connections with the press to counteract; forty egos to assuage.

Godin blew so much air through his nostrils that flashes of grey-white light appeared before his eyes. What had happened to Scotland Yard? Didn't they realise that he had a murder suspect and no ordinary murder suspect at that; and a murder suspect scheduled to leave the country within the next twenty-four hours? He tried Scotland Yard again. His fax machine came to life; and the slow appearance of the crest of the Metropolitan Police in London told him that Scotland Yard had delivered.

Godin read the fax line by line, and Will Chaucer too, came to life, filling Godin's head with mixed emotions and more questions than ever.

But did he now have enough to arrest? Were his suspicions confirmed? He read on. The depth of analysis was frightening; the content was simply unbelievable; but enough to arrest and charge? No; enough to arrest on suspicion and interview? Possibly.

Godin checked that Chaucer was still with Surette. Observing officers confirmed that the only movement was the arrival and the departure of Surette's wife. Godin estimated the number of officers he needed. It was to be done discreetly. If the press got wind of an arrest, with the possibility of release without charge, then he would look like a fool. Four officers - that was all.

Godin was back on Royal Street. Chaucer would suspect nothing. Godin was nervous. Most killers, as Olivier Godin well knew, were of limited intelligence. Chaucer, on the other hand, had a brain; an intellect beyond most - far beyond the average murderer for sure. Godin prepared himself. Surette suspected nothing. Chaucer suspected nothing.

"William Xavier Chaucer - I am placing you under arrest on suspicion of the first degree murder of Darius Trémé and Mia Laval."

In seconds, Chaucer was gone; gone from Surette's study; handcuffed to Olivier Godin, booked then interned in the bowels of the New Orleans Police Department.

"You may sit or you may stand, Mr Chaucer."

"Godin I presume," Chaucer announced, "you seem to have been following me around for a couple of days - Whites yesterday morning; the Coffee Shop opposite Surette's office; and up and down Royal Street on my way over to Bourbon. Then there was your elongated visit to Whites last night. Do they pay you to be incompetent, or do you offer incompetence free of charge?"

Godin had suspected that Chaucer had made him. If Chaucer knew he was being watched, why not turn around and declare it?

"I didn't think you were going to let me down; and thank you for appraising me with your sarcastic wit. Forgive me - I thought wrongly that English humour was pointed and worthy. Thank you for the clarity."

"Wrong; there was no humour in my reply. That was not humour. It was a statement of the obvious. Are you going to charge me?"

Godin tried to hide his disappointment.

"Not yet; a few things first."

"My bet is that you have pieces of paper from England; and the supposition that comes from assisting Surette. Then there was my manufactured disappearance in The French Quarter yesterday. It isn't very much is it?"

"You can assume that I wouldn't pull you in on the basis of supposition. It is amazing what friends in low places can do for you - friends in Scotland Yard."

Chaucer began making connections, categorising what Scotland Yard would and wouldn't be able to send to Godin.

"You, have a serious past," Godin exclaimed, "serious indeed. With a past like yours, we have every potential to keep you under lock and key within the limits of the law, before we consider charging you. A swab first, if you please."

Godin produced a cotton bud from his pocket and asked Chaucer for a sample of his saliva. Chaucer's DNA would be compared to the DNA at the crime scenes.

"Why don't you level with me? If you do have access to Scotland Yard, you'll have found not one reference to me as a criminal - far from it. I have an unblemished record. I have never been arrested and have had minimal dealings with the police in a personal capacity."

"Is that so?"

"Yes"

"Well; technically yes, I suppose. But it isn't quite the whole truth is it? I am aware that you do not have a record; I am aware that you have never been arrested. That doesn't mean you haven't been under investigation."

Chaucer remained silent.

"Yes; your stepmother - missing, presumed dead; has been missing for a number of years; whereabouts unknown. She went to work one day and didn't come home; didn't get to work; hasn't been seen since despite a massive police search over a number of years - foul play suspected but nothing ever proven."

"Rumours Godin; rumours. The woman's disappearance was a terrible shock for the whole family, especially my father. As for my stepmother, it was no secret that we didn't get along."

"Whether you got along or not, you were under suspicion and she is still unaccounted for. And your alibi was never very strong, was it? Your alibi on the day he went missing was a statement from your wife that you spent the day at home with her in Oxford. This brings me on to the subject of your wife."

"The subject of my wife is closed - is a closed subject. I refuse to discuss it here and I will refuse on every occasion to talk about Anna. Understand?"

There was a knock at the door. The open door unveiled Eveny Brien and standing behind her, Roux Surette. Godin knew; the rules had changed. Not only was Chaucer subject to scrutiny; so now, was he. But what did he have to lose? He went straight for Chaucer's jugular,

"Your wife."

"I told you I would never discuss my wife."

Chaucer glanced at Surette.

"I told you before I will not discuss what happened to my wife. This is difficult enough already."

Godin continued - happy to see Chaucer rattled.

"What I have here in my hand is a piece of paper that details all that happened to your wife and all that your wife did. It is not pretty reading; but I am not going to read it to you in full. We can't waste time. The shortened version is for the benefit of my boss and this mealy psychiatrist who seems infatuated with you."

Godin pointed at Surette. Surette almost didn't notice, so eager was he to listen to what Godin had to say.

"Look; is this absolutely necessary?"

"Yes I'm afraid it is."

Surette settled himself. Chaucer sat on the edge of his chair.

"What we have here is the story of how your only wife, Anna, was stalked by her father wherever she went, after you were married. This is a transcript of a police report setting out Anna's descriptions of how she was continuously followed by her father and how, during her childhood, he subjected her to physical and sexual abuse. This document goes on to describe a man whose desire to control couldn't deal with the fact that Anna had found a man who loved her and a man who she could love."

Surette moved closer.

"So what did Anna Chaucer do? How did she act having reported the matter to the police, knowing there was little they could do? Well, one day, when you were at work, Anna Chaucer got into her car and drove the fifty miles or so back to the house in which she grew up - the house her father lived in with your wife's unknowing mother. Anna waited outside until her mother was out. Once he was alone, Anna Chaucer let herself in and found her father asleep in front of the television.

By the time he had woken up it was too late. What followed was a litany of torture and savagery inflicted upon Anna Chaucer's father bearing precisely the same hallmarks as the evisceration, mutilation and murder of Darius Trémé and Mia Laval. Then, having completed what she set out to do, Anna Chaucer drove home, documented all that had happened to her and the reasons for her actions, took out the revolver she had stolen from her father's desk drawer, put the barrel of the gun against the soft flesh at the roof of her mouth and fired a bullet into the base of her brain. A couple of hours later, you returned to a house surrounded by the police, who had found your wife's body along with a note explaining what she had done to her father and why she had chosen to torture him in precisely that way - precisely the same mechanics of torture inflicted upon those children.

Let me summate - we have you, a man abused by his own stepmother, according to the not so confidential medical records the English police were able to dredge up; we have a woman who subsequently disappeared from the face of the earth, with you being exonerated by your wife's alibi; then we have your wife, who tortured then executed her own father before ending her life with his revolver. We then have your appearance in Surette's office on the day following the death of Darius Trémé - a man off the street; a stranger with a past which puts you somewhere ball park in relation to the deaths of two children, murdered using the same technique as your wife used on her father; and we have more than that. You have conceded that you avoided our surveillance yesterday at or near to the time Mia Laval was killed. You have a history of mental illness necessitating many excursions onto the psychiatrist's couch. And you claim, as far as I can see, to have the inside track on who and what the killer is and why these murders are taking place, which is novel, for a man insane enough to kill these children would in my estimation be similarly unbalanced enough to try and play with the very same people appointed to try and catch the killer. One final thing - you are booked to leave the country tomorrow morning which struck me as extremely convenient timing - almost too convenient. You have to admit, these are creatures of circumstance and actuality which would tend to suggest iniquity."

"But you have no motive Detective - you have no motive."

"Do we need a motive with crimes of such sickening madness? Is there anything rational in what has been done to those kids?"

"I may have a guilty mind. But I need a physical presence too. All you have is circumstantial evidence. You have nothing that puts me at the scene of either crime. So; are you going to charge me or can I get on with what is left of my life?"

Godin hesitated. He cast a glance at Brien.

"If I could have a word with you in private?"

Godin and Eveny Brien stepped outside. Godin explained his position.

"You have to admit that there are pretty compelling reasons for having this man kept in the station and questioned, regardless of what Surette says. If Surette had not been involved, no one would have batted an eyelid if I brought a suspect in and held him until I was satisfied. Chaucer seems to have got into the psychiatrist's head. For two days - two days, ever since Darius Trémé's body was found, Chaucer has been stuck to Surette like glue. Two days ago they had never met each other; now they are conjoined."

Godin looked at Brien for understanding. He found nothing. He felt desperate.

"Look; can we at least compromise rather than letting this man go? Why not - we insist that I accompany the Chaucer and Surette; that I am allowed to sit in and satisfy myself? I could control Chaucer, who is a suspect, and, I could evaluate their discussions."

Brien was to the point.

"Stay with them. I'll force Surette to agree. You'll stay by their side until Surette thinks they have finished. But do not try and interrupt. Sit and listen."

Godin felt some semblance of relief. As he turned to go back into the interview room, Brien stopped him.

"Good work Olivier. In a moment, I'll leave you to it."

Explain it as he may, Surette could not convince Brien otherwise - Godin was to accompany Chaucer until Chaucer was on an aeroplane heading back to London, or charged with first degree murder. Either Surette accepted the arrangement or Chaucer would remain in custody and Surette denied access to the man.

"So; I am free to go?" Chaucer asked.

"No; you are not free to go; you are technically free, yes; but you are only free in the sense that you are to continue to assist the psychiatrist."

"And Whites?"

"You are allowed to play Whites tonight but only if I attend Whites with you. If you go to the bathroom, I will be going to the bathroom with you. Whatever you do, I will be attending with you."

Godin smiled; Chaucer smiled back; and Surette watched - watched as Chaucer's stupid grin annoyed him, as it had done so often before.

XXV.

The house was empty; and Surette explained - Emily was teaching; the children were with their mother. Surette's home was theirs for a couple of hours.

Chaucer had not intended to tell Surette of Anna's death and the way that she had died. He had not expected it to be advertised by Godin. The desire to help had now mutated into the need to justify the past to Godin, not Surette. Chaucer had grown tired of Roux Surette; and he was irritated by Godin. Anna's end was but nothing compared to the tragedy of her life. Respect should not lead to resurrection; yet Chaucer was resigned to defending his wife; and his past. He was the only suspect they had.

Godin, on the other hand, felt cheated - cheated by Roux Surette, who had put himself before the needs of the dead. It was Chaucer's doing; and he needed to know what kind of hold Chaucer had over Surette. What had come from the Englishman's mouth that had forced the irrational reactions from reputedly a measured and careful man? Surely, the answer was now at hand.

Godin, Chaucer and Surette stepped into Surette's study.

"Do you mind if I take a look around?"

Without waiting for an answer, Chaucer paced the room, interested in Surette's book collection. Godin sat down and made himself comfortable. So did Roux Surette.

"You have some very interesting books here - and so many. You have such a vivid interest in history. That Blackstone's Commentaries on the Laws of England take your fancy, or the criminological works of the French philosopher, Michel Foucault, is almost perverse; some pretty serious stuff here if I may say so."

Surette wasn't aware that Chaucer had studied Foucault. Godin wasn't aware who Michel Foucault was.

"Criminology at Oxford, Godin; tedious."

Chaucer continued looking at works of philosophy, social science, anthropology and psychology. Next to these were the important political and social commentaries of the sixteenth and seventeenth century in French, German, Italian and Latin. And there was an extensive collection of general historical literature, most of it concentrating on the Middle Ages and the Renaissance.

"Very off the wall Surette. I didn't realise you had such an overwhelming interest in the past."

Surette didn't have much of an interest in the past. History was in some small part interesting to him. He couldn't speak German or Italian, his French was Cajun and his Latin was sparse. He found philosophy dull and impractical; psychology was plainly something he had studied but theology was for the unknowing. Psychiatry was his enduring passion and apart from a few tomes, the books Chaucer took interest in did not belong to him - they belonged to his wife, Emily.

"So history is your wife's passion; and the other books represent her interests? This is most enlightening."

Enlightening indeed, Chaucer thought, for he had read most of the books which lined Surette's bookcase and while they provided intellectual stimulus for the select, they were books not meant for the masses.

Surette considered his first question. He looked at Godin, inconveniently sat in the corner of the room. He looked at Chaucer; he thought of Chaucer's wife. He thought of his own wife and his young children. He thought of Mia Laval and Darius Trémé. He thought of himself.

Chaucer ignored him.

"It seems to me that we need to return to the rhyme again for it is integral to this matter."

Godin listened intently; Surette effected distance.

"First the Trémé boy was killed and this note was attached to the boy's body - a rhyme; a riddle; something to interest; something to test - something proximate to identification; then what happens?"

Chaucer looked at Godin.

"This time a girl and this time essentially the same agencies of torture and murder save for one difference - Mia Laval was decapitated and her skull spilt open to reveal her brain. The same note but another body; the same message and a killer thinking that there is sufficient in the rhyme; so what must we do now?"

Surette didn't know. Chaucer feigned impatience.

"We need to see what else is relevant. We must survey the remaining lines, for in the latter lies our best chance of understanding the author."

Surette took out the rhyme from his pocket. He made two copies and handed one each to Chaucer and Godin. Chaucer read the last four lines aloud.

'Returns the knife to normalities cocoon -

Nourished with applause,

Feeding upon urban epitaphs -

The reason not the cause.'"

"I want to consider the idea of 'nourishment.' A man who has succeeded in killing two innocent children believes there is nourishment in applause. But what nourishment is there in the censure and admonishment of an entire community? How can repulsion equal applause? The killer of those children must be the most despised human being; so despised in fact that language cannot do justice to the depth of hatred most feel for the creature who murdered Darius Trémé and Mia Laval. Is nourishment correct?

I hold the view that it is. We are not dealing with what most consider acceptable. Nourishment to the ordinary mind is not sought in wickedness; yet nourishment to the twisted psyche arises exactly because wicked actions demand and receive the revulsion of the moral majority. Social repulsion sustains the killer. Murder becomes appropriate and torture becomes germane.

The killer is milking the surrogate limelight because the killer has spent many years repressing urges to kill. Now that these urges are out in the open, it is a matter of salivation every time the nourishing evil of his actions come to light. Nourishment is the sum total of all moral censure for what the killer has done …. 'returning the knife to normalities cocoon' …. as it says here, is the completion of an assigned task with a successful outcome.

This is, from one perspective, insanity personified. This is but one perspective. What is insanity if we have a regimented agenda, a purpose, a reason and pre-ordained outcome to considered actions and the anticipation and emotional superstructure that comes with trait and reflective capacity? Maybe the outcome represents insanity; maybe insanity is turning the world of meaning upon its head. The killer is, as I have told you, sophisticated. And the juxtaposition of inverted meanings and planning suggest reflection and reasoning. They suggest control. We are looking for an intelligent specimen – a specimen to all intents and purposes normal; but someone with a dark - a hideously dark past."

Chaucer looked at Godin.

"This is the reason I had Surette get you to look at all of the people who knew Darius Trémé and won his trust. You should be narrowing matters down to a few names. You should run those names through whatever computers and databases you have. The answer, in my opinion, is somewhere in there."

Godin mentioned the blanket DNA tests on all connected males; he also confirmed that a reduction exercise was being undertaken. Godin's brain was, however, at a tangent. It was obvious that Surette was blind; it was obvious that it had been Chaucer who was defining the killer. Surette was merely a mouthpiece for this potentially murderous Englishman; and murderous besides, Godin could see that Chaucer made sense. But Chaucer would make sense if he had committed these crimes and composed those words himself. If Chaucer was not culpable he was the only individual with something meaningful to say.

Chaucer, on the other hand, could not stop thinking about Surette's books. It was a long time since he had read several of the tomes on those shelves but there was something about them which struck him as important. He couldn't quite put his finger on it; he couldn't quite remember why a collection of old words should pose important questions.

"We need to move on. The last few lines of this rhyme again - they are absolutely crucial; convoluted meanings bringing us closer to the mindset and the proclivities of the author."

Will Chaucer read them out loud once more...,

"'He feeds on urban epitaphs -

The reason not the cause.'"

"Strange; really strange and related to the concept of nourishment - the idea of feeding upon a response; an epitaph; the content of this message is something the killer wants chiselled onto his headstone. This is an extremely vain individual but a clever one - a man who had been able to see within to the motives and urges driving him in the years before he was a killer.

The killer will seek and find solace in what people will say about him. By the deletion of existence at the top of the tree, he was making more room for those below. Maybe the point is, by taking a life he was creating the space into which could ascend another whose opportunities would have otherwise been limited. Rather than taking life, the killer is simply making room for others."

Surette was puzzled; something didn't make sense. Chaucer was contradicting himself. The killer knew both victims and their families. Chaucer had assumed the killer was from the same social epoch as the victims. Why then would the killer be looking to the ordinary to congratulate him on creating room for someone of a lesser social order to succeed? What kind of 'nourishment' was that? Why 'feed' on the censure of all and play to the gallery of the majority?

Chaucer was prescient.

"Why would an upper class killer feed on lower class utterances as to the purported gravity and outrageous immorality of his crimes? Let me spell it out for you - the killer may be interned in a higher social strata now; but it wasn't always like that. This is a man feeding on urban epitaphs because this is a man whose background is entirely urban; whose psychological malady is the fruit of a poor urban upbringing. This is a man who seeks in some sick and twisted way, the approval of his childhood peers - childhood being, incidentally, the period when the abuse which this man was subject to, manifested itself. So, perversely, he seeks the disapproval of his peers within the social group in which he now resides, to mean approval, but mistakenly imagines the actual approval of the urban majority where a lack of economic and social achievement are the norm. A socialist might call it killing for the people. Factor that into your analysis. You are looking for someone whose past is one of a lower epoch shall we say, or is someone of whom very little is known as to their past."

Godin made a note. Chaucer resumed.

"So, finally, we come on to the last line -

'....the reason not the cause.'

Chaucer looked at Godin and Surette expectantly. Neither Godin nor Surette spoke.

"I'll explain then. Question - what is the 'reason?' Is it the same as asking the question - 'what is the cause?'

Difficult to distinguish I think, between the two. It is probably impossible. If we imagine there are no objective truths and that language sometimes gets in the way of understanding, the last line of this rhyme becomes crucial, not as a way of offering further information which may help you catch this killer but as a way of understanding his thinking.

Why the reason and not the cause? Well, in one sentence, very simply and following the environs of the human mind, a man may know the reason he undertakes a course of action but he may not be able to establish why he was imperilled to act in that way. Let us say we have a man who is what we call a homosexual. Forgive my circularity but the reason he is labelled a homosexual is because of his relations with the same sex. The homosexual will in all likelihood agree with the label, with whatever moral connotations it has. Then ask the general observer of the 'reason' for the label. The general observer could say the reason this man is a homosexual is evidenced by his actions. But ask the general observer what is the 'cause' of a sexual preference for men and one is on entirely different ground. See?

Ask the same question in relation to the killer. Why label him a killer? Why is he a killer? Simple - it is because he has killed, knows he has killed and knows of the immoral connotations of the label. But what is the 'cause' of his predilection to kill? If the killer argues that he is not the cause of death because he had no choice, that is, his choices are predetermined for him, then he is trying to obviate blame as well as making a statement as to the origins of behaviour. The reason he is a killer is evidenced in his actions; but the cause of his need to kill is something else. The 'reason' and not the 'cause' suggest to me that the killer is trying to absolve himself of temporal responsibility for if one cannot define the origin of behaviour, one cannot allocate blame by labelling outcomes."

Rubbish, Surette thought; wordplay. Godin agreed.

"But it isn't nonsense gentlemen. Or is it? We are not dealing with a fool. We must assume that the last line has some meaning. And the killer is making a conclusive statement as to the origin of his own pathology. What the man has done is to state categorically that responsibility for his actions lies not in the chain of events - the actuality which culminated in the deaths of Darius Trémé and Mia Laval; no. Responsibility for their deaths lies in his essence, for want of a better description. And as he cannot control this inviolable need as he has no choice but to kill, therefore he is not responsible at all.

Yes; his essence - the need to hurt, kill and maim is the essence of the man. That is the reason he kills - his essence. A chain of consequentiality stems from what this man simply, is. All that happens is what lies at the locus of man. Each of us has a unique fingerprint that we cannot erase. This man's needs are something he too, cannot erase. By looking at his essence, which he believes he cannot change - the innate; that given; the inviolable stubbornness of simply having no alternative, the killer absolves himself of responsibility because he cannot escape. He has come to terms with what he is; and who can allocate blame to a man who has decided that he is pre-ordained and imperilled to act in a certain way? The cause of the reason he has killed?

We shall never know. Why we are what we are, is the insoluble fact of human existence. The killer chose to display Mia Laval's brain. Within the brain lies the cause of inescapable predilections. These predilections are unexplainable as they are unique. Physicality is all he has got. "

Surette contrasted a killer without choice in opposition to Chaucer's ability to assuage his violent nature through music. Chaucer was the lucky one. His inner talent for music had helped him find peace. As for the killer, there was nothing within to effect release, save for to kill.

Godin thought of the killer; and of himself. The similarities between his feelings and the murderer's mind left him with no other choice. The parallels were disturbing knowing that he was a man who denying his sexual essence, comparing himself to a killer who had released his. What was the difference, save in outcome?

Then there was the rhyme as a template of life itself. For whoever grasped its meaning; whoever could decipher the proclivities and the essence of its author, seemed welcome to expose the murderer's identity. Not his temporal identity - not his name; his job; his status; his past - no; but his essence; his being; the secrets as to who and what he was. In Chaucer's exposition of the killer, he could see others beyond the veils, the shields and the justifications; the constant battle between essence and control. Godin pitied the killer. He pitied himself. How a conspiracy of genetics and environment had disserved them both; and how the killer had now disserved the environment. Godin resolved to learn; Godin would learn the killer's lesson. He would not hide from himself anymore, nor would he repress his needs. He would not imperil anyone to understand but he would not shy from explanation.

"Like I have said, the last line personalises the killer's identity. And the killer has made a bold philosophical statement as to the very nature of personality itself. This is a man who thinks more deeply; whose emotions and feeling are switched on entirely to those around him. This is a man devoted to the question as to why the world humankind has created has worked against him and works at all. What, the killer asks, is the cause of his differences? What and why? "

For Roux Surette, all was now over. Chaucer had finished making him think. The man's brain and its power and knowledge were all past tense. Chaucer looked at his watch and told Godin that he had to leave as he had to be in Whites. Before he left, Chaucer returned to Surette's books.

"Can I borrow these?"

Chaucer picked out a number of volumes in no particular order.

"Thank you Doctor. You know I am playing tonight - my last night. Why don't you return to Whites? I would like to have the chance to say goodbye to both of you."

Chaucer stood to leave. Godin stood also, and slid his notes into his briefcase. Roux Surette did not stand, as he did not notice their departure.

XXVI.

Godin had a profile of the murderer and all he needed. Chaucer had returned to Whites. Redundant; spent - Roux Surette took stock. For the first time in his life, he understood that no matter who had listened and acted upon what he said; in spite of the public status and respect; regardless of how many people his search for excellence had pushed aside; and despite the self-proclamation as special, ascendant and potent - a caucus of respect and worthy of jealousy; he was ordinary - basic even; and little more than average. Perhaps - just perhaps, he was luckier than most, as he had a vocation. But his was an ordinary life imitated by the multitude, and he would drift into middle age then into retirement having created nothing, developed nothing, propounded nothing and been nothing that hadn't been defined before.

The last two days had opened his eyes; had opened his eyes to possibility. Chaucer was a man who had changed the fundamental tenets of his being; had fundamentally altered the chemical and nurtured synthesis and created himself anew from the rottenness of his instinctual self. What will; what power; what strength - strength embedded in childhood and colouring an entire life.

What a mind the murderer must have, too; strength to isolate and quarantine urge, desire and want. These men - the Englishman, Will Chaucer, and the man who murdered those children, were removed from the miniscunality of all that Roux Surette had ever known. Indeed he was, small; he felt, unworthy - his ordinariness made him unworthy. Triumph didn't come from adversity; adversity allows innovation to flourish; and growth ensues - no adversity; no innovation - ordinariness.

Surette hated himself; hated himself for not being something special; and different. The rubicon of realisation was crossed; and he wished he had been denied full passage. The flip side was much more attractive - a living purgatory but a human idyll, was eminently preferable; Hell even, and not purgatory - where all motive and urge are clear given the short sighted contentedness of trinkets and toys, status and illusion, smoke and mirrors, confusion and the constant fulfilment through the vacuous - careers, family, children, money, status, pride and perpetuation.

Just to be different for a day; Chaucer for the day; the murderer for an hour - Surette grew tired and bored of his own vacuosity. Honesty had become dull and he wanted delusion. But he wanted depression too; he wanted insight; he wanted experience.

Selfish; there is no right to happiness - he was abusing the privilege of contentment itself. What had he become? Roux Surette wanted what he could never attain - understanding. Understanding can't be bargained over, or bartered; but lies in the hideously complicated retinues of emotion, perception, intuition, reasoning and analysis, environment, experience and talent. Without this elusive combination, all is a tardy palace full of cheap furniture and fake trinkets. Surette felt the seeds of depression growing within, a state brought on by greed for the insidious and the profound learning curve upon the delivery of pain. He was trapped; encapsulated permanently in an environment he wanted to escape from; and the one environment he wanted escape from was the one environment which offered him solace because he was unable to escape.

Surette left and strolled the streets of The French Quarter, as he did every day. He looked at this unique American melting pot - The Quarter; and he thought of all the people it had thrown up and sent forth. Most were benign; deluded maybe, but benign. How was it possible here, of all places, for a killer to contain that kind of anger within? How could the killer conceal all of that pain in a life marked by ordinariness?

Someone must have noticed. Someone close to the man would have grasped the iniquity within - a wife or a child would have sensed a tapestry of acceptability worked over urges to destroy and the need to emasculate purity; or was love, blind? And if the perpetrator was married to a woman who knew little of darkness, how would she know what was within and hiding. No such woman could; nor could any man. But what had triggered the need to kill? What had flicked the killer's switch? From where was the emanation of blood-lust which characterised this man, secured from? How had circumstance tapped the killer's veins and the killer's urges to destroy and invalidate life itself? And would the answers to that question ever be apparent should the killer be caught?

What lay in store for him, now that his eyes had been opened? Where could he go now that the cosy bubble of convenience and achievement had been exposed as the flimsy, porous structure that it was? Would it remain or would it fall?

XXVII.

Godin was attending to the boredom of isolating individuals who knew Darius Trémé and Mia Laval, as Chaucer went through a sound check with his band. Godin periodically looked up and all seemed well; but Godin could not have guessed that something was bugging Will Chaucer and all was not, well.

It was those books – Surette's books; it was to do with crime and punishment and something to do with his past. He kept looking at the pile of Surette's books on the table next to Godin. He blew a couple of long notes on his trumpet, and let off a Dizzy Gillespie riff, just because Dizzy Gillespie riffs were his favourite. He played for five minutes, which was long enough, and put his trumpet back into its case. He thanked his band. At last, he got to look at the books he had taken from Roux Surette's study.

It took ten minutes. All he needed to do was to skim the relevant sections - just catching sight of the relevant sections was enough to remember what they dealt with and where he had seen them before. It was so simple. It was so difficult. The consequences were so horrific.

Memory pounced; and the pain returned - for Chaucer had seen his wife reading these very books in the weeks before she had killed her father. Each described, for different purposes, the ritualistic character of torture and murder prevalent and accepted in medieval France and England. Now there they were on prominent display in Roux Surette's living room. It all made sense.

Chaucer considered her manner - the stillness; the awkwardness; the inquisitive eyes; the coldness; the stilted and difficult language; the way she had devoured his playing; the way it had got to her more than anyone else; her husband's embarrassment; how unaware he was of her potential to act like that; how stupid he had been; how absurd it seemed that he couldn't recognise in the flesh, the very characteristics he had spent so many hours explaining to her husband. Emily Surette. He had to be sure. He looked at Godin.

"Emily Surette - would she have had the confidence of Darius Trémé and Mia Laval? And the children's parents?"

Godin looked at Will Chaucer as if he were mad.

"Just answer the fucking question."

Godin felt cold, immediately. According to his team, Emily Surette's name was the one name that kept cropping up, as the only name who had access and confidences. But she was a female and outside the brief of expectation. They were looking for a male. And the idea had seemed so absurd that they had dismissed it - Godin, too.

"Read this. Read it and tell me where this book came from."

Will Chaucer showed Godin various passages detailing torture, evisceration, death and their rationale during the latter stages of the medieval period in Europe – but before punishment for sin led to incarceration and a clean death - back to a time when death was a public process and the populace watched the body being systematically destroyed.

"I have to use the phone. We need to establish where Roux Surette is."

Godin handed Chaucer his cell phone. Chaucer stepped outside Whites and called Surette's home number. No answer.

"Quickly; tell me - how long before Emily Surette lets out the children she teaches at school. How long is it before they go home?"

Godin looked at his watch.

"About now."

"Are you convinced?"

Chaucer pointed at Surette's books.

"Look; we don't have time. Work it out for yourself - read; read. This describes the old English statutes that regulated and documented the minutiae of torture and execution; and this French book describes how the French and Italians meted out the same horrors upon their people. My wife read these books before she killed her father. The same mechanics of murder and torture were inflicted upon Darius Trémé and Mia Laval. Those very same books are in Roux Surette's study and what do we really know about his wife? What do you really know about his wife save that she is a teacher, and is the one name that keeps popping up as someone who would have the trust of both Darius Trémé and Mia Laval. Then take her manner; trust me - she fits. This woman fits."

Chaucer tried Surette one more time, and failed.

"Must have turned off his telephone - he will be in his office; he will be in his office, sulking."

Godin was still reading. With each sentence he knew that here was a perfect template for torture; and murder.

"Convinced?"

Godin nodded.

"We could be too late. You said school has just let out for the evening?"

"Yes it has - no more than five or ten minutes ago."

"Christ," exclaimed Chaucer "You know what she will do now don't you? She has only one choice left."

Godin jumped out of his chair, grabbed Chaucer, pulled him onto Bourbon Street, and the two men ran through The Quarter in the direction of Surette's house, with Godin holding his Detective's badge in the air.

"We need to get to Surette; we need to get to his office. She may stop if she sees him. Is there no faster way of getting there than through these drunken crowds?'

Godin picked up a couple of uniformed officers along the way, and ordered them to clear a path. Most tourists were oblivious; a few intuitive natives were helping. Godin and Chaucer reached Surette's office; Chaucer broke open the locked entrance with his shoulder and found Surette fast asleep on the psychiatrist's couch. As quickly as he could, he tipped Roux Surette onto the floor.

"Grab him Godin and drag him if necessary. And don't explain a thing to him before we get there. Just grab him."

XXVIII.

Roux Surette had no idea why he was running; he had no idea why he was running toward his own house, until it came to him - where was Emily? She was supposed to take the children home. How could she leave them alone with what was loose in The Quarter?

"Have you got a key?"

"There's no time - strong-arm the door."

"Ready?"

Godin and Chaucer hit Surette's front door with their shoulders at the same time and the wood splintered into pieces, forcing Godin and Chaucer to fall. Before they got up, Roux Surette was over the top of them. Chaucer feared the worst. Godin was beyond resignation.

"Doctor; please don't go in there."

But it was too late, and Chaucer - slower to his feet than Olivier Godin, who had drawn his gun, followed them into Surette's living room. Directly in front of them stood Roux Surette - motionless; and in front of Roux Surette stood Emily Surette, holding a large red-hot knife to the throat of their eldest son, Alex, who was unconscious, naked and hanging alongside his brother, David

Blood was oozing from a deep wound on Alex Surette's shoulder. The stench of boiling sulphur and wax in the room was overpowering.

"Stay back or I'll slit his throat."

Godin pointed his gun at Emily Surette's head.

"Put the gun down Detective - he'll be dead before your bullet hits me."

Roux Surette didn't notice that Godin had a gun, nor did he notice where it was pointed.

"Emily?"

Emily Surette remained silent. Her mouth was contorted; as if she was trying to chew her own teeth; and her dead eyes were unblinking, lifeless, insect black and expired.

"Emily; is that you?"

Neither Godin nor Chaucer moved. Nevertheless, as Godin pointed the gun at Emily Surette, Emily Surette held the knife to Alex Surette's throat.

"Yes; it is me; Yes, Roux; this is truly me. This is the monster you married. This is the woman created by forces and reasons beyond even your simplest imaginations. Yes; it is me. You thought you knew me?"

Emily Surette did little to hide the contempt in her voice.

"Well; you thought of nothing, Roux. You always thought of, nothing. Call yourself a psychiatrist? The only reason I married you was because I thought I could tell you. And all you ever did was tell everybody else what to do - you never examined those closest to you. A man with all the evil of the world for a wife; the mother of your children, and you never noticed. No one ever noticed me."

Emily Surette bared her teeth.

"Well you have noticed me now haven't you? All of you have taken notice now. And God knows how I tried to get you to notice me. God; how I said so often things which would have made a man of ordinary intelligence think. But you thought of yourself as beyond the ordinary, Roux, and so became less than ordinary. And I became trapped. I, was left alone to look after these two bastards - left to watch them look at me and rely on me every fucking day of their puerile little lives - loving their mother and never ever knowing how much I wanted them dead in case they end up trapped and alone and an adult with nothing but contempt for the world and hatred for everything in it.

They will pay, just like the others for whom life had the potential to be easy. They will pay in physical pain one millionth of the mental pain I have had to suffer all of my life. If I couldn't have what my children will have, then they will not have it either. Neither will any child. They shall all die execrable deaths."

Chaucer saw Godin's finger squeeze the trigger of his gun.

"Escape; that is what this is about - no; it is about release. This is about release."

Emily Surette looked at Chaucer and smiled.

"At last - someone comparable; a kindred spirit; someone I can relate to.

"Music; jazz; feelings - a kindred spirit because I touched you last night; the first time you had ever been touched - music which wormed and meandered its way past your defences? You know nothing of me, Emily. The signs of understanding that you heard, do not harm; they do not hinder; and they do not have me kill. Although I too release, if I touch it is because others allow me to - they choose to allow me to. You however, give no one else the choice. And you assume that I am a kindred spirit?"

"Precisely."

"Then why am I here; why are you holding a knife to your son's throat?"

"Answers."

"What answers?"

"Answers to the question."

"What question?"

"*The* question."

Chaucer raised his voice.

"What fucking question is that?"

"The question," Emily Surette paused, "the question, is why."

"The question is not why, anymore, Emily. You have already answered all the questions you could have asked given what you have done. You will serve no purpose by taking these lives. Your purpose here is spent. Your purpose here is spent because your statement has been made. The poem exposed your vanity, your past, your secrets, your sufferances, your pain and your desire. You have nothing left to prove for you have answered the question yourself. The answer to the question is that no one knows the answer to the question. The question was never meant to be answered. Your downfall is that you never realised it. No one knows why we are what we are. The cause of your drive is beyond words, and is beyond knowing. Taking away the life of these children does not expose the cause of your need to kill. You cannot punish the body for the sins of the mind because the mind isn't culpable; and the mind must be, culpable. You cannot absolve yourself of responsibility because you claim not to have had the choice. The reason you are a killer is because you chose to be. Why you need to kill is an unsolvable mystery. What causes the need to choose is beyond science. I pity you. You are unlucky. Whatever has happened to you; whatever the genetic lottery gave you and no matter how the circumstances of your past add up to this moment, you cannot absolve yourself of this sin and you cannot absolve yourself of the desecration of innocence. You chose to kill. Now you must choose not to kill. You feel contrition; you feel shame. As much as you want to harm, your feelings are trying to convince yourself not to. Be strong as you once were and do not give in."

Emily Surette looked at her husband. Briefly a look of shame, a look of humiliation and a look of remorse passed across her face.

"This is what I am imperilled to do. What am I if I am not my true self? I am nothing. I am what the rest of the world has made me. I am what the rest of the world wants me to be. This is what I want. This is what I have to do. Do you think I have regrets for what I am? I know I am evil. I have no choice for I am innately evil. Why evade the truth? Why sit and watch as I have done all my life, seeing the lucky ones never questioning why they are, while every second of this miserable fucking existence I have been left to rue the day I was made, not knowing why I was made this way nor the causes of my needs. I was born to kill and the lucky others must be born to suffer. And when they die and when I am exposed, I will be able to tell all - to tell all of you who never question what we are, that only by asking the question can the cause of evil be eradicated. The emasculation of innocence is the gateway to the understanding of evil. And I, am the lodestar of understanding."

The knuckle, holding the knife, turned white. Emily Surette gritted her teeth and attempted to slice open Alex Surette's throat. Godin went for the trigger and Chaucer went for Emily. Roux Surette produced a revolver he had extracted from a sideboard drawer. His first bullet hit Emily Surette in the left temple and the force and direction of the bullet swung the arm, which had already drawn blood from Alex Surette's neck, away from his body. Her temple was obliterated.

His second bullet hit Emily in the heart and there was a muffled thud as her lifeless body fell to the floor. Chaucer, shocked but in control, took Emily Surette's knife and cut down David and Alex Surette. Each had a weak, a very weak pulse. Chaucer lay David on the floor and wrapped a throw around him. Godin did the same with Alex. Outside, with an ambulance waiting, Godin and Chaucer picked up Alex and David Surette and laid them in the back. As they did so, Roux Surette's mother, who had pushed her way through the growing crowd, insisted on going in the ambulance with her grandchildren. Roux Surette's father was escorted by Godin into the living room where Roux Surette stood, transfixed, staring at his wife's body. It didn't take Surette's father more than a second to work out what had happened. Surette father grabbed his son, threw his arms around him, and led him to another place.

XXIX.

Will Chaucer didn't want to play Whites, that night. He wanted to go home, to Oxford. All he could think about was Anna - his wife; all he could see was Anna's smile. That night, Will Chaucer dedicated his performance to the memory of 'Anna.'

Chaucer didn't see Roux Surette sitting at a table in the darkest corner, furthest from the stage. He never saw Roux Surette order a Scotch on the rocks, nor did he see him look into his drink, lost and in pain - somewhere to recover; somewhere to reflect; somewhere, to think.

All Roux Surette did, as he sat in isolation, was to let the haunting beauty of Chaucer's playing flow over him. He never noticed what Will Chaucer was wearing; he never noticed the audience - whether they had tears in their eyes; what colour they were; what they were; were they were from. Roux Surette was a sleepwalker, dead to the world; dead, to all.

For the first time in his life, Surette realised without realising it, that language would never do. Through pain; through suffering and through loss, Surette realised why only music mattered. Roux Surette had realised what music and what jazz, was for. For at that time, only the power of music mattered. Only music mattered. Only jazz, mattered.

XXX.

Chaucer called for a cab to take him to the airport. Five minutes later, Chaucer heard the sound of a horn. He picked up his suitcase and his trumpet, checked that he had his passport, airline ticket and checked out of the hotel.

"Thought I'd give you a ride; best to make sure you'd gone."

Godin was standing next to a New Orleans Police Department squad car, clad in standard patrolman dress.

"The lift is appreciated but the sentiment is confusing."

Godin smiled.

"See; we have a big problem in the States with illegal immigrants - Mexicans, Africans, Chinese and Japanese, as well as others looking for a new life in this old frontier. When you can make sure they are going, you make sure they are going. You know how it is."

"Strange to see a Detective in uniform. Have you been demoted?"

"Ceremonial today; demotion isn't an option at the moment - after yesterday my reputation is on hold. Everybody is too shocked to think."

"And Roux Surette - with his parents; or with his boys?"

"The boys are in hospital. They are alive and they will live. Both had every limb dislocated, David's right arm was broken and Alex had a chunk of flesh taken out of his shoulder. It will be several months before, physically, they will be back to normal."

"Is Surette speaking?"

"No; hasn't said a word, poor bastard; hasn't said a word."

As they heading out of The French Quarter, and through New Orleans, Godin and Chaucer spent the next twenty minutes in silence. Eventually, Godin pulled up at the set down point of Louis Armstrong New Orleans Airport, stopped the car and turned off the engine.

"Really Detective Godin; I am alright from here."

"I'll be seeing you through the gates if it's all the same; see - I'll be with you until you enter the legal immunity of the international lounge."

"Why Detective; why?"

"Because something about this whole thing stinks and I am not sure what it is. Something about you is not right."

Chaucer smiled.

"I just can't put my finger on it."

Chaucer looked at his ticket and the small queue that led through passport control to the departure lounge.

"Emily Surette never did admit to killing that little girl, Godin. It was the death of that little girl which really flushed her out. Anyone knowing the mind of the killer would have known that. But there again, who in reality, knows the mind of a killer except a kindred spirit?

And who can flush out a killer except a kindred spirit?"

Chaucer passed through customs and Godin watched him go. By the time Godin had deciphered the potential myriad of meanings within the Englishman's last few words, Chaucer was next in the queue to board the plane back to London, smiling as he went, wondering whether Godin understood ambiguity.

Godin understood Chaucer all too well; and he knew that he would never know if the Englishman had killed his stepmother, who was still missing, or that he had killed Mia Laval, with the assumed murderer, now dead.

He did know that Emily Surette would be cited in perpetuity as the murderer. Her DNA was eventually established at both crime scenes; but she did teach the victims and DNA was suggestive, not conclusive. It didn't absolve Will Chaucer. Nor could Godin implicate Will Chaucer, anymore. For now, William Xavier Chaucer, had gone.

XXXI.

Godin drove back to The French Quarter, and drawing up to Police HQ, noticed the unmistakeable figure of Eveny Brien standing outside. She looked worried.

"Your father has taken a turn for the worse; you need to go to the hospital."

With Eveny Brien beside him, Godin turned on his police siren and sped toward New Orleans University Hospital. As he rushed into his father's room, he realised he was too late, as the continuous monotone of the heart monitor next to the bed told Godin that his father was dead. One last time, Olivier Godin looked into his father's lifeless eyes. But this time he did not speak; for this time, his father could not hear.

Gently - as gently as he could, Olivier Godin closed the lids covering Jack Godin's redundant eyes. Olivier Godin was now alone. And in that moment, Godin made the decision to come out and unveil the inner man. He had nothing to lose and nothing to gain. What difference did it make - he would survive, so - yes; he would be honest - yes; he would be true. Damn the consequences. Damn, all.

Oliver Godin left the hospital; and as The French Quarter surrounded him once more; as familiarity crept up on him and demanded a return to the ways things had always been, Olivier Godin sighed - yes; he wanted to come out; alas, he knew, he could not.

www.ingramcontent.com/pod-product-compliance
Lightning Source LLC
Chambersburg PA
CBHW050522260626
47157CB00004B/1438